SHADOWS IN THE FOG
A Block Island Tale

By Tecla Emerson

OutLook Press
210 Legion Ave. #6805, Annapolis,
MD 21401
TeclaM@aol.com

Dedicated to Adeline,
(one of my favorites)

The loneliness you get by the sea is personal and alive. It doesn't subdue you and make you feel abject. It's stimulating loneliness.

~ Anne Morrow Lindbergh,
Gift from the Sea

~ CHAPTER ONE ~

The mourners, grim faced and mute, stood in the morning fog. The misty grey swirled in silence around them. Each, in turn, glanced over at Molly. They were tight-lipped, with a hard knowing expression piercing their cold New England eyes. Young as she was, she knew the memory of that scene would never leave her.

There was an open, wet scar of dark brown that cut through the earth. It was harsh in the otherwise green field. There were flat white blooms of Queen Anne's lace mixed with golden rod. All were a bit droopy from the moisture that had floated in with the fog. But what she would remember most vividly were the drops of mist that had settled on the end of Pastor Bleakman's nose, and how he stood like a statue not wiping at the accumulating drops. Instead, he let them drip on the curling pages of his bible. The cover was cracked; and if one inspected it a bit more closely, the print was faded and the pages yellowed with age. The Widow Grady stood next to Molly, her voluminous black bombazine dress spread like a grand protective circle, daring anyone to step on the yards of dark fabric. It smelled of camphor and stale cabbage.

Molly leaned over and plucked a sprig of the yellow flowers and held it to her nose. She sneezed and wiped at the dribbles with her sleeve. Before, Grams had always slipped a clean hanky in her pocket; now there wasn't one.

"Ashes to ashes," said the Pastor. Widow Grady slapped at the flower knocking it from Molly's four-year-old hands. Her eyes held sadness as she watched the blooms fall into the mud.

"Stand still, child," the Widow hissed down at her. Molly, hands cold from the dampness, pulled her sleeves down and gripped them like mittens over her fingers. She watched as the pallbearers lowered first one, then the other, of the identical rough pine coffins.

It was just yesterday when Molly had gone to the wake, where one after another of the towns-people filed through Grams and Paps parlor to stare at the pine boxes.

"Caught in a nor'easter," the townspeople said, "Shouldn't 'a been out in it." Molly hung back, but she heard them talking. "Wanted to get back to their Molly," she'd heard the postmis-tress say as she dabbed at her eyes. Her fingers were stained by ink from a lifetime of stamping envelopes. "First time they'd spent the night off island since taking the child in those few years ago."

"Such a tragedy," murmured Mr. Littlefield. His limp slowed his walk as he passed by the two closed coffins. One after another of the town's people filed past the hastily crafted pine boxes.

Mrs. Littlefield shook her head and said over and over, "Oh my, oh my," which was the extent of her conversation as far as anyone had ever heard. "Oh my, oh my," she said again as if for emphasis.

"Why're they closed?" a girl with long braids and upturned nose asked her mother. Her voice pierced the stillness of the room.

"Coffins are always closed," her mother had answered, "when it's a drowning."

Molly had stood back in the corner listening and watching. She knew most of the town's people, if not by name, then by sight. Odd how they were all a bit stooped, and most seemed to be an allover grey color, even though today they all wore black.

"Poor child. Now what's to become of her? Who'll care for her?" It was Mrs. Tuttle. She looked down over her pince-nez, her eyes were sharp and clear. It was the only youthful part of an otherwise bent and tired body. She of course knew the answer to her question, they all did.

"Widow Grady, I'll be sending some cakes by now and again to help out," said Mrs. Bainbridge as she pushed back the strand of hair that refused to stay tucked under her black snood, "'til maybe they can locate someone to take her permanent like."

"I knew your adopted Grandparents well," said a man as he hobbled past on his cane, his hair flowed into his beard, giving him the look of a goat that had been caught in a briar patch.

"They never adopted her," said Widow Grady.

"I know that, but what else can you call them?" he said, his voice cranky with age. "They're all she knew." He took a moment to clear his throat, coughing into his handkerchief. "If they hadn't taken her in, she'd have been in an orphanage on the mainland and who knows what would've become of her."

"Humph," said Widow Grady as she helped herself to another piece of pie. "Wonder where she really came from," she muttered under her breath.

"I remember the day they brought her over from the mainland on that Kaposhkin woman's boat," he said raising his voice to share his story with the others. "She was just a mite of a thing. She wasn't much bigger than one of those cod you all pull in come spring."

"We know, Mr. Brooks, we all got to see her, if I remember correctly," said Mrs. Marlowe as she turned to Molly. "You were some tiny, I'll tell you. Smallest baby I'd ever seen." Molly, not sure what was expected of her had continued to swing her legs back and forth. Someone had lifted her on to a high stool where she'd been told to sit and be still.

"Molly, say good-bye," said the Widow Grady

pulling her back from her memories, and back to the yawning holes at the gravesite. Molly looked down into the dark holes cut into the muddy soil. The Widow pushed her forward, her foot crushing the blooms that had been knocked from her hands. The mist that the morning fog brought in was quickly turning into rain. Pastor Bleakman had closed his bible and stood staring down at her, his nose looking much like the prow of a boat when it had been upended.

"But where're Grams and Pap?" she asked, her brows coming together forming an almost straight line. She looked up at Widow Grady.

The woman stared down at her new charge, her jowls all-atremble. She clicked her tongue against the roof of her mouth, letting out a "tsk-tsk," as she pulled the child back. "In the box, you foolish child."

"But Pap couldn't fit in that box," she said. It was true. Pap had been so tall that it had been necessary to lay him on his side and bend his legs up to make him fit. Of course the undertaker, Mr. Grimsley hadn't shared that information with anyone and wasn't about to. He never attended the burial of one of his "clients," so he didn't hear the remark. Most often it wasn't necessary to curl up any of his "clients" that way, but then they weren't all quite so tall. Of course, there had been that time with "Smokin' Joe". There was only one way to fit him in the box, but Mr. Grimsley never talked about that. He had done what he had to, nailed the top shut and then quickly put it out of his mind.

Widow Grady's four sons lined up behind her, poking at each other while trying to stifle giggles.

"Hush," said the mother to the boys. "Stand back now," she said to Molly.

Molly watched as the gravediggers threw in shovelfuls of the earth, each one heavier than the last. As cold as it had gotten, there were beads of sweat forming on the foreheads of the two burly men. One looked over at Molly; his hooded eyes sent a shiver down her spine.

People began leaving. Each walked past her and looked at her curiously as if she were some unknown debris dragged from the sea.

"What's to become of her," said Mrs. Bainbridge, as she shook her head. It wasn't a question but a statement that there really wasn't much anyone could do with one forlorn little girl who had no one but the Widow Grady who would care for her.

Mrs. Littlefield murmured, "Oh my, oh my," as she dabbed at a tear, but then rushed by, anxious to get out of the rain. It was starting in earnest, the drops beating on the ground.

Widow Grady pulled at her arm, "Come along now. Don't be dawdling." Molly, pulling her sleeves further down, managed to cover most of her fingers. Mindful of the mud and rocks they walked with some caution down the path. Rivers of water squiggled around them.

Molly, not bothering to lift her skirt, walked behind the huge bulk of Widow Grady. She turned her face up to the sky and stuck out her tongue, catching raindrops. They taste like tears, she thought.

The path was slick beneath her Sunday shoes. Intent on catching as many raindrops as possible, she paid little attention to her footing; until suddenly, and without warning, one foot flew out ahead of her. She had slipped on a piece of loose shale. As she began her tumble to the muddy ground, a strong hand reached out and caught her, carefully righting her.

"Molly," said a voice, the accent unmistakable, "here now. Up you go child." The woman set the young girl to rights and patted her arm. "I'm sorry for your troubles, child." Molly looked up into the eyes that were nearly lost in the aged face of Mrs. Kaposhkin, Block Island's only fisherwoman. "Knew yer Grams and Pap well," she said, her eyes warm as they took in Molly. "You be needin' anything, child, you find me," she said pointing to herself.

"Humph," said the Widow Grady, grabbing Molly by the arm. "Come along now." She pushed Molly forward. "The child won't be needing any of your help."

The rain started to pour down and began to blow about in the northeast wind. Molly could hear the screech of the seagulls as they fought over tidbits pulled from the sea. She shivered. Drops soaked through her dress. She could feel them winding in rivulets down her back. Turning once, she looked back to see Mrs. Kaposhkin watching, her hands deep in the pockets of her canvas apron, her pipe unlit between her teeth.

The four Grady boys caught up to them, leaping over puddles, down the rock-strewn path, pushing, shoving, and tagging each other with glee. Making their way down the lane and up the path, they approached the house at the end of

Cemetery Street. It was grey. Age and neglect had left their mark. Raindrops splattered on Molly's cheeks. She gnawed at her lower lip, staring at the place where she was to live. It was the same color as the overcast sky. Even at the age of four she was able to recognize the lack of care. Shingles were missing. Two of the second story windows poking out of the eaves were cracked. The bottom windows were overgrown with vines. The front walk had weeds growing up between the broken bricks. One of the shutters, caught in the breeze, was banging unheeded against the side of the house. Not at all like Grams and Pap's house with its always shining windows, its neatly trimmed walkway and tidy flowerbeds.

"Go on now. Get on in there with them boys. We got a meal to prepare and it's not gonna' fix itself." She gave Molly a push through the door, into the gloom.

Peering around the interior, her eyes adjusting to the dark, she took in everything. It had few pieces of furniture: a table in the center of the room, one leg propped up with a brick, a bench set against the wall, a butter churn, the dasher broken off at the end, and a spinning wheel pushed into a corner. There were four stools of various heights around the room. One chair was pulled up to the hearth. Stuffing leaked out of the cushions. There was but one flame struggling to stay lit in the hearth that was heaped with ash. The bit of light it shed added little warmth to the drabness of the room.

"Coats hung here," said Widow Grady, pointing to the nails haphazardly sticking out of the wall. Two of the nails were badly bent, letting the coats slip to the floor. "We'll get your things later," she said. Waddling across the floor, she let out a great sigh as she lowered herself into the chair near the hearth. "The boys sleep up attic. No reason why you can't sleep up there too," she said, pointing with her thumb to the ladder that led up to the trapdoor in the ceiling. She'd had her own room at Grams and Pap's house, a place just for her, where she belonged.

Molly looked around the room, she shivered once. Shifting from one foot to the other, she felt a warm trickle as it ran down her legs. She watched in fascination as a puddle formed around her feet, darkening the floor. Grams hadn't been there to tell her to use the loo before setting out this morning.

She heard a whoop and a cry of disgust from the woman sitting in front of the hearth. Molly, unaware that she'd pulled the sleeves of her dress down to completely cover her hands, heard or felt, she wasn't sure which, the stitches on the sleeves begin to give way from the strain.

She looked down at the stain on the floor and wished there were some magic that could swallow her up and make her disappear forever.

~

CHAPTER TWO

"Here, Molly Anne, I can help," Jack said. He took the handle in his hands, hands that had grime permanently imbedded around the nails. He cranked the handle, winding the rope around the spindle. "I'll get it." He leaned in and retrieved the wooden bucket. "C'mon, I'll walk you back up to the house."

"Jack, I can do it," she said. "Your Ma's going to get mad if she sees you."

"I can deal with her," he said, with all the bravado of a fifteen year old. He looked over at her, his black hair falling in his eyes. "You don't think I'm afraid of my own Mam now do you?" he asked. His eyes twinkled as he smiled at the thirteen-year-old girl. She looked down, smiling slightly, grateful for the help. The bucket was going to be difficult to carry without sloshing it all over her skirt. Wouldn't matter anyway as it was threadbare and already badly stained. She wanted to tuck her skirt up to get it out of the way but knew that would be further cause for the Widow to become angry. It had been almost ten years since the Widow had taken her in and she knew only too well what could spark her anger. Molly still could not understand why the Widow Grady was always so annoyed with her.

"Are you going to the beach later?" he asked. "I'll come too if you go." The beach, she thought; wouldn't it be nice to just go to play and meet friends and splash in the water like many of the other Islanders? She'd only done that once that she could remember and that was years ago when she lived with Grams and Pap.

"I will be going today actually," she answered. "I know your Mam wants me to bring a load of the moss to town. She says we're low on just about everything and I need to get something traded or we'll all starve." She didn't mention that the Widow said it'd be her fault if they all had to go without, 'cause she hadn't brought in enough of the Irish moss after the last two storms.

"I'll help you collect it," he said, "and the last bunch you brought in is near done, isn't it?"

"It is that, but we need another couple of days of sun to get it really bleached. Littlefield's won't take it unless it's near snow white and they've got the best price." They talked easily as they walked along together, she smiling slightly, while he held the bucket, trying to keep it from sloshing. "If the weather holds I'll have it done soon enough and it may even be as much as three or four pounds."

"Ma will like that," he said.

"Hmm," said Molly, "I'm not so sure."

"Well of course she will. She likes when you bring home money."

"She always says it's not enough."

"You know what she's like. That's just her way."

"Why did she decide to take me in Jack, when Pap and Grams died?" The question spilled out before she even thought out her words.

"Probably," he answered, as he readjusted the bucket sloshing a bit on his bare feet. "Probably," he started again, "'cause the town said they'd give her money to care for you. She's had no money since my Da died. We've had to live off whatever we could trade for, and real cash money sounded awfully good to her, and she needed the help," he said. "It's a houseful of hungry boys," he said and tried to laugh. "Her legs are paining her some and she sure needed an extra pair of hands." He stopped and looked at her. "Molly," the intensity of his eyes bored into her. "She doesn't hate you. You know that. It's just her way."

"Jack," yelled a voice at the door of the ghostly grey house. "Didn't I tell you to bring in a load of peat? What are ya' lollygagging for? Get it in here now." Jack handed Molly the filled bucket and winked at her from under his mop of dark hair.

"I'll see you later," he said. She gave him a half smile in return and took the bucket.

"Yes Ma, I'm going right now," he said heading off in the direction of the bogs that held the peat, or tug as he liked to call it. There was such effort in pulling it free from the bed where it had formed, that most of the boys on the island called it tug!

Molly walked carefully up the path strewn with rocks and bits of broken shells. She tried not to slop the icy water and, at the same time, tried to think of a way to get around the woman blocking the doorway.

"Get in here, LooLoo," she said referring to Molly's accident so long ago when she'd forgotten to use the loo. "My land, a girl who can't even control her water, how're you ever going to do anything right and keep yer'self out of trouble?"

Molly steeled herself for the blow that she knew was coming. True to form, as the Widow Grady stepped out of sight of anyone who may have been outside, including Jack, she slapped Molly on the back of her head. Molly bit back a cry. Rarely did anyone witness the slaps that were doled out whenever it suited the Widow. Rarely did anyone see the bruise or mark that was left by the slaps.

"Get that water boiling now or we won't be eatin' 'til the middle of the night. Then, LooLoo," she said, using the hated nickname. "Then," she continued, "get that stew together. It 'pears to me that you haven't even bothered to get this floor swept. Can't you do anything right?" She raised her hand to slap her again, changing her mind as she heard the slam of the door and the voices of two of the younger boys. "James, Joseph," she said in one breath, "you two get on out of here and help your brother with the tug or we're not going to be having any fire tonight. Where's Mack?" she asked. The door slammed in answer.

Molly, tears threatening to spill over, moved out of arms reach and over to the hearth, trying not to slop any of the water on the floor boards that had been worn smooth by so many feet. Tipping it, she carefully poured it into the kettle suspended over the fire. Only a bit of it sloshed on the hearth. It sizzled as it hit the hot bricks. She moved back quickly to get out of reach of the hungry flames. More than one cook had met with disaster when her long skirt had brushed too close to the hot coals.

"Now what are you doing, you clumsy girl?" asked the Widow. Molly tensed, waiting for the next blow. Two arthritic legs didn't allow her to walk about too often, but when she was up and about she was a force to be reckoned with. Molly would try to think of reasons to be outside; either to work in the garden, or fetch the tug, or work at drying the seaweed. The Widow was not as much of a threat when she was sitting in her comfortable chair in front of the hearth. It was too much of an effort to come up out of her seat to strike Molly, so instead she would let her tongue do the lashing.

"Here's the tug," said Jack surprising them both. His footstep was light and more than once he'd startled everyone by suddenly appearing. He placed the heavy crate next to the hearth; it was heaped full of the squashed oval blocks of peat.

"Don't look quite dry enough to me," said Widow Grady, her voice carrying its usual irritation.

"Of course they are Ma, I wouldn't bring in wet peat, now, would I?"

"Don't be smart-mouthing me, boy, or you'll be feeling my belt across your backside."

"Oh Ma," he said exasperated, but left it at that.

"Where'd yer brothers get off to?" she asked as she lowered her bulk into the chair at the hearth. It creaked in protest.

"They ran down to the dock, Ma, waiting for the *Deliverance* to tie up."

"And why, pray tell, did they go down there? Don't they know they have work to do?"

"You remember Ma, the Doc is due in today. They want to see what a man with one arm looks like."

"If you mean that Brewer boy, he's no Doctor. What are they bothering with him for? With only one arm left he's not gonna' be doing much doctoring."

"Oh, Ma. Who knows! I'm going down to the dock too, and Molly's coming with me."

"Oh no, she's not. Just who do you think's going to cook dinner if the two of you go running off all over the island?"

"Well, you could, Ma."

"Don't be fresh with me boy," she said rising up out of her chair. It took some effort, but she rose up to her full height and crossed her arms over her ample bosom. "You go down there and tell your three brothers to get on up here if they're plannin' on eating any dinner tonight." Standing had taken more effort than she expected so lowered herself back into her chair.

"Oh Ma," he sighed, knowing the futility of arguing. He grabbed his hat, took one quick look at Molly and fled out the door. He'd see her later when they went to collect the seaweed.

Molly couldn't help but think how much she would have liked to run down the path, through the town and down to the dock with the boys. In the past they'd had wonderful fun during the rare times she was able to get away. They'd chase each other with a game of tag or play hit the ball with a stick. She'd become a fast runner, thanks to the games they played. Jack said people were going to start calling her a regular tomboy.

The times were few and far between when the Widow Grady didn't notice she was gone. Every now and then, if she were in a benevolent mood, she would allow Molly to go to school, but it was rare. The Widow, more often than not, had some reason why she would have to stay home. For Molly, school was more of a problem than it should have been. She loved the days that she could go, but it was difficult to keep up with her class work. Miss Ames, the teacher, seemed to understand and didn't push her unnecessarily. Instead she always was sure that Molly had books to bring home to read, which she was careful to keep out of sight.

On the days that Molly returned from school, it was almost as if she were being punished for going. The Widow had done nothing all day except dream up other chores to be done; and no matter how well Molly washed the floor, or the windows, or mended the boys' clothes, it was never done right. The Widow would take the opportunity to berate "Looloo," and slap her again, usually with her hand, but sometimes she used the straw broom that she kept close by.

Was this to be her life? Would she ever be free or would she ever again have a home like she once had with Grams and Pap?

~

~ CHAPTER THREE ~

The town never questioned the Widow too closely as to why Molly was rarely in school. Whenever anyone did ask, she'd say either she was ill or Molly was ill or there were errands that needed to be tended to immediately. The excuses were never challenged. No one paid much attention. Most thought she was old enough to no longer need school.

On days when the Widow would keep her home, she'd send Molly off to pick up seed at the store or the bit of flour that she would trade for. Some days she'd send her down after a storm to collect the Irish moss washed up on the shore. Then it was Molly's job to dry it and bleach it, and bundle it up, and take it down to Littlefield's. Most of it was then sent off to the mainland. It was a prized ingredient for a pudding, but the ladies also said it could be made into a cream that they insisted could be used to make their skin soft.

Molly only knew of the island people using it in a pudding and that the Widow used it as a method of obtaining money. The solitary walks along the beach in search of the seaweed was most often a fine time to be alone, which was pleasant enough, but she knew not to share that with the Widow. She was sent often enough as it was a means to trade for food or to sell what she'd collected.

Molly never missed the opportunity while she was there to collect shells or rocks or other bits of mysteries from the sea. She would fill her pockets with the treasures tossed up from the wild and turbulent waters. Some shells she could identify, others were a mystery. Her special box in the corner of the attic was nearly filled with all the many intricate and different shells that she'd found.

Today she was anxious to get away. The weather was fine, and though she wanted to go to the docks, the beach would be a fine escape. Maybe when she got the stew together, and the corn bread mixed, she'd be able to sneak off and run down to the town before the Widow even noticed and then run back to the beach for the moss.

It had been years since she'd moved in with the Grady family; and rarely did she have time to be by herself. The Widow seemed to always be standing over her watching whatever she did. Molly sometimes wondered if she disliked her so, why did she keep her? There were enough mouths to feed already with her own four boys.

Jack at fifteen had started adding to the food pantry by fishing with Mr. Davies. He most always brought home something, be it cod or mackerel or blue fish. Sometimes people at the dock would give him a one-clawed lobster for their dinner, knowing how the family was always struggling for food. The one-clawed lobsters didn't sell well when the fishermen brought them to the mainland to sell.

The garden was tended by the three younger boys but it was rare when any of them even set foot in it. That is except Mack. He was the youngest of the four, and had the biggest appetite. It was hard to fill him up so he'd sneak in to steal a cucumber or some of the fresh ripe tomatoes. Then he'd deny it even with the tomato drips still fresh on the front of his shirt.

As the youngest, his mother was easiest on him. Molly was left to do the weeding and hoeing and planting. It was well known that Widow Grady had a difficult time controlling her boys. It was easier to press Molly into service with whatever chores the boys had left undone.

"Go on down now and get that seaweed before the tide comes in and we lose it all," she said, coming up behind Molly.

"Yes Ma'am," Molly said, addressing her in the way she'd been instructed. Molly was delighted, although she was careful not to show it. The Widow thought she was punishing her. Molly picked up her basket and tried to put on a sad face and not rush out the door. It'd been days since she'd had any freedom at all. With the storms that had come in during the week she'd been housebound, and now here she was free for what was left of the afternoon. No sooner was she was out of sight of the house, than she grabbed up the hem of her skirt, tucked it under her belt and began to run.

She breathed in the salty air. She didn't even mind when her braids came undone, leaving a stream of blonde hair trailing behind her. She ran the whole way down to the Grady's area of the rocky beach. The islanders were very particular as to which part of the shoreline they were each allowed to scavenge. Molly knew well to stay in her own area. Stopping for a moment, she caught her breath, her chest heaving from the long run and breathed in the freshness of the salt air.

Standing just above the lapping water, she took a moment to watch the ebb and flow of the water as it spread over the sand. In moments only, it would slip back to where it came from, taking with it bits and pieces of shells or pebbles. Larger waves would toss up pieces of debris and then pull them back in the retreating waves, never be seen again. Of course there were days when the waters would pound so fiercely that nothing was safe; rocks, sand, shells, boats and even people if they weren't careful. More than one fisherman or unsuspecting boater had been lost in the violence of a passing storm. The day was wonderfully bright and the beach was littered with the seaweed that they called Irish moss. It was after a storm so the pickings would be effortless, an easy afternoon to be sure. During the rare times that the Widow made her way down to the shore, she had Molly go in all the way up to her waist to pull the slick bits of moss off the rocks. It was always icy cold and the moss was slippery in her bare hands making it hard to handle. But, it didn't matter how cold and icy the Atlantic was, if there was moss to be had the Widow would see to it that they were going to get it. It was the one way that she could bring in money with little effort. Of course she wasn't the one wading in to the frigid Atlantic or reaching down into the chill waters to retrieve the treasure. Today, though, Molly was on her own, without the Widow yelling instructions.

Pulling off her leather boots, she wiggled her toes and stopped to listen a moment to the music of the ocean. It was always changing, from the soothing slow song of lapping on a calm, fog shrouded day, to the thunderous crashing during a nor'easter. Today, after last night's storm, the ocean had calmed. A gull glided overhead like a kite on a long string drifting silently on just a breath of a breeze. Sparkles from a brilliant sun danced on top of the waves like shimmering fairy dust. Molly breathed in deeply, enjoying all the scents that drifted through the air. She'd forgotten her bonnet, but no matter, she was as brown as an Indian already from forgetting it too often. The sun had streaked her hair with the lightest blonde and her sun darkened complexion set off the intense blueness of her eyes.

Today it was almost too easy to fill her basket as she wandered back and forth along the stretch of beach. Seaweed from the storm was pushed into piles where the tide had dropped it. Even more was draped over the rocks, hanging at odd angles. Her bare feet delighted in their freedom even when an occasional broken shell pricked at her unprotected soles.

"Molly," said a voice pulling her back from deep within her own thoughts. It was Jack, back already, carefully balancing his pail and his clamming fork. "Can I help?" he asked.

"No, I'm fine." She'd very nearly filled her basket and just in time. The tide was rapidly creeping up, reclaiming the bits and pieces that had been ignored. "Look, the bucket's nearly filled and there's enough more so's I can finish it. I'll help you instead, and did you meet the boat?" she said, all in one breathe.

"Yeah," he answered, "But there was no Doc. Guess he got wind of it and saw all of us standing there so he didn't get off the boat. He must be some freak or something with only one arm."

"Can't imagine a Doctor with just one arm," she said.

"He's not going to be a Doctor. Heard he only came back here to hide out. He's been gone so long; he thought no one would remember him. He's going to go live on his parent's old farm and do nothing. His parents left him some money," he said stooping to start the process of digging up the elusive clams, buried deep in sand. Molly put down her basket and as Jack dug with the rake, Molly would reach into the hole and pull out the clam.

"You O.K. Molly?" he asked noticing how quiet she'd become.

"I'm fine, just enjoying the day," she answered as she bent to pick up an unusual coral colored shell. It had one small corner broken off. "Look Jack, I don't think I've seen one like this before." She held it out for him to see.

"No, don't think I have either. It's certainly different. There's a flaw. Do you see it and will you keep it?"

She laughed, her rare laugh that Jack loved to hear. "Of course, you know I save all of them," she said. "Look how pretty and intricate it is. How can something this unusual not be worth keeping, flaw and all? This one will go on my window sill."

"Here Molly, hold it up to your ear." He held the curved shell out to her. "What do you hear?"

She laughed again, her blue eyes twinkling. "I hear the oceans of some far off place." She paused a moment listening intently. "A place where I would like to settle and call home, maybe a bit too far to ever get to, but a beautiful place. Maybe where the sand is a brilliant white, a place so far away we could never reach it, try as we might; and if ever we did, it would only mean we were lost and then may not find our way back again." There was a sadness that had crept into her eyes. "But, then, not finding our way back? Maybe that would be good. Here," she said holding it out to Jack, "What do you hear?"

"Oh," he said, his brow furrowed in concentration, "I hear far off lands too, with lots of big trees blowing in the wind, but you might be right, we'd be lost and maybe would never find our way back again, and that may be bad, I'm not sure." He handed the shell back.

"I'll keep this one always," she said. He

laughed. He felt suddenly awkward and dug a toe into the sand. Already she'd nearly filled one large box with the treasures she'd found tossed up by the mighty Atlantic. This new treasure would be one of the many that she had collected.

"You're going to need the entire attic if this keeps up," he said.

"Well then, you four boys can just all move out and let me have the whole attic for myself." She smiled over at him as she pushed the stray curls out of her eyes.

"Well, there's only one of you, and far as I can see you've taken over most of the attic as it is."

"Not true, and you know it. But I thank you, Jack, for making a room just for me." It wasn't quite a room but it was the only place in the house where she had a little bit of her own space. Jack had hung up what was left of a tattered old quilt. It went from one side of the narrow roof to the other. She even had a window, which the boys were happy to give her. The boys were content sleeping next to the chimney that came up the side of the house. In winter it was so much warmer staying near the bricks that had been heated by the fires of the day. In summer they dragged their mattresses over to the other window to try to catch a breeze. Molly's window faced east and after she'd given it a good scrubbing, she could enjoy greeting the morning sun that streamed through, bringing warmth and light. And then many a night, when she couldn't sleep, she would listen to the waves pounding the coast of the little island, while gazing out the window at the night sky. She would dream of a life apart from where she was, a different life, but she hadn't decided what that was exactly.

The best part of the attic room was that the Widow was so large she couldn't fit through the hole in the ceiling to get up there. Fact was the ladder probably wouldn't hold her weight anyway. They had privacy in the attic, though the Widow could hear whatever they said and when she wanted their attention she didn't hesitate to bang on the ceiling with the fireplace poker. This would often happen in the middle of the night when she wanted Molly to get up and fetch something for her. Some nights when Molly would read by candlelight, the Widow would see the glow shining through the cracks between the floorboards. Then she would yell out that whoever had the light best quit wasting her precious candles. Molly would be forced to blow it out.

"Here Molly, I'll race you back," Jack said pulling her back to where her mind had wandered. He took the filled basket. It held not only the Irish moss, but the almost perfect pink shell cushioned in the middle of the bed of seaweed.

Molly took one more deep breath of the salt air, as she gazed towards the west. The sun had begun its descent into the sea. She wanted to fill up with the beauty of the day. Was there a way to capture it so's it would never end? Walking slowly at first, she picked up her pace, then began to run in Jack's direction. "Wait for me. I'm coming," she called out. The retreating figure turned and stopped. He watched as she ran to catch up.

~

~ CHAPTER FOUR ~

"Loo Loo, that moss looks about ready." The Widow stood in the pathway, her arms folded across her ample bosom. It was one of those rare times when she left the safety of her house.

"Yes Ma'am," she said. Her fingers were crossed behind her back as she made a wish, "Please let me go down to the town." It had been too long since she'd last escaped the confines of the house and yard.

"There's not much of it so pack it up and take it on over to Mrs. Bainbridge. She likes it now and again for those puddings she makes. Trade it for a ham for our dinner." She turned back to the house. "Be quick about it now – you hear?"

Molly knew she'd never get a whole ham out of Mrs. Bainbridge for such a small portion of the

Irish moss, but at least she'd get to walk over there.

"Molly, where ya' goin'?" It was Mack, the youngest of all the Grady boys. He ran to catch up to her.

"Bainbridge's," she answered, knowing full well he'd want to go, too. Much as she would enjoy an afternoon to herself, someone to walk with would be nice enough, she decided.

"I want to come," said Mack. "Wait up, Joseph and James are right back there," he said, pointing to the odd shaped tree house that they'd recently banged together.

"Aren't you all getting a bit old for climbing trees?" she asked.

"Those two are, but not me. Maw still won't let me work, so what else am I goin' to do?" He kicked at a rock that refused to become dislodged and muttered a quick "ouch."

Joseph and James ran, panting to catch up to them.

"If you three can't behave," warned Molly, "don't come with me. If you're bad I'm telling Jack and he can deal with you. Understand?"

"We're not gonna do anything," said James who, at thirteen, was the same age as Molly, but he seemed much younger.

Molly walked ahead, ignoring the pushing and shoving that went on behind her. She listened for a while to their chatter, which consisted mostly of senseless babble. "Hey Moll', ye' suppose old Jim Bone's gonna be about?"

She smiled. They were being foolish and didn't really need an answer.

"He might come and snatch you up," said James.

"Ha," she said, not really wanting to be drawn into the conversation.

"Heard he's eaten more'n a hundred little kids," said Joseph, followed by laughter.

"He's just an old Indian," said Molly. "He never hurt anyone."

"Jack said," added Mack, "That he'd come after us with a tomahawk if we didn't behave. And that he's scalped bunches of people!"

"He was fooling you," said Molly. "And where is Jack today?" she asked.

"...Would've come," said Mack "if he knew we were going to Bainbridge's, but he's out on the Jones' boat, fishing."

"Too bad for him," said Molly. "I know he likes the horses."

"He said one day he's goin' to come over and ride that big grey one," said James.

"I don't know about that," said Molly. The horse farm came into view.

"I like the dappled one," said Mack as they approached the fence. The horses, instead of walking over to greet the visitors, either ignored them or walked away to the far side. They'd had enough encounters with the Widow Grady's boys to know it was trouble when they were around.

Mack bent to pick up a stone. "Now never mind that," said Molly, "Why not just leave them be. I've got to go up to the house, and it's not going to do to have all her horses upset by you hooligans."

Mack tossed the rock from hand to hand. His two brothers came up behind him. "What are you a scaredy-cat?" they said to their youngest brother.

"Leave him alone, you two. I'm going this way, you can either wait, or I'll see you at home." Remembering the few times that Molly had walked over, they remembered how Mrs. Bainbridge had given her a plate of cookies to bring home. They decided to wait.

Molly walked on, glad that they'd decided not

to accompany her. They weren't bad she'd decided, just mischievous. They were forever knocking over fences, teasing farm animals or punching and hitting each other. It became tiresome after a point. They needed jobs she thought, something other than sweeping out Littlefield's store on Saturdays or when they occasionally helped to clean a load of fish. None of them ever did a very good job, except Jack. He was the only reason any of them did anything. It was his idea that they should each have some work but it was hard to get anyone to hire one of them except when no one else was available to work. They didn't have the best reputation for completing anything.

Molly rapped the brass knocker against the door. She was sure Mrs. Bainbridge would be in. It was said that in all her years, she'd never left the island and rarely ventured beyond her property. She seemed happy raising her six horses. Her children were long gone to the mainland, and her husband was confined to a wheelchair.

"Well, hello Molly," she said as she pulled open the door. Mrs. Bainbridge was stooped with age, but had clear, bright eyes. "What brings you here on this sunshiny day?"

Molly held out her basket, "I've Irish moss here if you'd like any." She was never quite sure how Mrs. Bainbridge felt about her or about the Grady's. She knew she never hired them to help; and whenever she met any of the boys, it was hard to miss her looks of disapproval.

"Yes," she said, not unkindly, "I could certainly use some for Mr. Bainbridge's puddings. He loves them so. Now I wonder if ten cents would be enough?" she asked. "There is quite a bit there now isn't there," she said, weighing it with her hands.

"If you had food to trade that might be of more use," said Molly, as she shifted from one foot to the other.

"Well now, I do have some hams that I'm near finished brining," she said. "I know the Widow is mighty fond of a good piece when it's freshly brined. Let me go see what I've got. Come back in the kitchen with me now. I'm sure I've got some cookies back there somewhere." Molly trailed close behind, her mouth watering at the thought of Mrs. Bainbridge's cookies. Baked treats weren't something ever prepared at the Grady house."Here, sit here." She waved a hand at the kitchen table. Molly looked around in awe.

The kitchen was an entire separate room with a huge hearth at one end and a massive cookstove set to one side. Pots were lined up on one of the shelves by size, from the smallest to the largest. The large one no doubt used to make some of Mrs. Bainbridge's delicious and well known soup. There were bowls and cooking implements on another shelf, more than Molly had ever seen.

"Here Molly," she said, putting a heaping plate of cookies in front of her. "And here, I've a bit of milk too." Mrs. Bainbridge was known for her cooking talents throughout the Island. She was one of the few people who could afford outside help but chose to do all the cooking and cleaning herself, using only Jim Bone, to help her with the animals. Everyone just assumed that because he was an Indian, he was good with horses. Course no one really knew who he was. He may have been a mute, Molly wasn't sure. Once before, when she had visited Mrs. Bainbridge, she had asked her why he never talked. Mrs. Bainbridge was the only one who seemed to have any dealings with him. Probably because he's not very happy had been the answer. She went on that he was one of the few surviving Indians on the island and all the land that you could see and probably the whole island had once belonged to his family. Now he was just a hired man. He was fine she added. He did his work without complaint. She had, of course, heard the stories and added that his eating children was simply not true. Of course he didn't. Molly knew that but had felt better after Mrs. Bainbridge had said it.

Molly was busy licking the crumbs from her fingers on her fourth cookie and drinking her second glass of milk. "Here now, I have a small ham. It should feed that family of yours for at least one meal."

"Not my family," said Molly in a voice just above a whisper. She wiped at the milk mustache.

"I know," said Mrs. Bainbridge as she busied herself wiping at imaginary crumbs on the table. "Do you ever wonder about your real family?" she asked.

"Now and again, yes, I think about it," she answered, her voice was low and it was hard to hear each word. "I remember Grams and Pap, but not so well anymore." A great sigh escaped, but she quickly covered her mouth with her napkin muffling the sound.

"I knew them," said Mrs. Bainbridge, feigning indifference. "Of course we all grew up on this island together; so naturally, we knew each other. They were fine people." She took a moment to shake out the rag over the sink. "They had a daughter, you know. Took her to the mainland for an odd illness that they said she had." She spent a moment searching through a pile of clean dishcloths and when she found just the right one, she wrapped the ham in it and set it in Molly's basket. "Odd," she continued, "How she died and all. I always felt that . . ."

A tinkling bell interrupted her. "Molly, that's Mr. Bainbridge, he's up from his nap. I've got to go see to him. Here, take these cookies." She tucked them into the basket with the ham. "Thank you for the moss," she said as she led Molly back to the front door. The tinkling sounded again. "He's not very patient, now is he," she said and patted Molly's arm. The door closed silently behind her.

Molly stood a moment on the porch and readjusted her basket. It was no surprise that she'd been nearly pushed out of the house. Although she'd never laid eyes on Mr. Bainbridge, she'd heard tell of him down at Littlefield's store. One could hear all sorts of things down there if one stayed long enough. Mrs. Littlefield could always be heard behind the counter with her "Oh my, oh my," with each new bit of gossip. No one had ever heard her say more.

The Bainbridge's were possibly the wealthiest residents on the island, and the most private, and the most talked about. Molly had heard down at Littlefield's that years ago Mr. Bainbridge had been thrown from one of his wife's prized stallions and never recovered. Mrs. Bainbridge had kept him secreted away ever since the accident and now she never left their estate. But everyone knew when that little bell tinkled, she ran to answer the call.

Molly looked down at the dozen cookies tucked snugly next to the ham and wished for a moment that they could all be hers; if she could just hide a couple from the boys; for herself and maybe one for Jack. She took three of the cookies and tucked them beneath the napkin. Wouldn't hurt a bit if the boys didn't know they were there. She turned in the direction to where she knew they'd be waiting.

~

~ CHAPTER FIVE ~

"What took you so long?" asked James, his voice close to a whine. "We thought you were never coming back."

"Got any cookies?" asked Mack.

Without waiting for an answer three pairs of hands plunged into the basket. James came out with four, Mack two and Joseph three. A fight began which Molly chose to ignore, she continued walking in the direction of home.

"Hey Mol," said Joseph, "Where ya' goin?"

"Home," she replied, "Your Ma is going to be looking for us."

"No, she ain't," said Mack. "She thinks it takes you a lot longer than it does to get over here, and we can take the shortcut back."

"Why don't we take the shortcut anyway?"

she answered.

"Well okay," said Mack, a spark of mischief in his eye. "Let's take the boat out. We've got some wind today." Molly knew he was referring to the old dinghy down at the old town harbor. It had been there forever with its one rickety mast and an ancient canvas sail that was repaired now and again by anyone who felt the need. Most of the town kids had used it to learn how to sail. Somehow it was cared for, never too badly in disrepair. It wasn't used very often anymore as it took some skill to negotiate the entrance to the old harbor, which had silted in from the winter storms. Most of the locals now used it only on a high tide.

"Come on Moll', let's do it. You've done it before."

"Well I don't know," she said. "I really should get back. And the weather could change.
She shifted her basket and looked up at the puffy clouds breaking up the blueness of the sky. Oh all right," she said, making up her mind, temptation overcoming good sense. "But not for long."

It took minutes only to untie the small boat as the four hopped aboard. James pushed off as Mack dropped the centerboard. Joseph, the best sailor of the group, hauled up the mainsail, and secured all the ties. Molly stashed the basket down in the hold and sat for a moment, her face turned up to the sun, enjoying the warmth and the feeling of freedom.

"Here," said James, "You take the tiller." Molly reached out and with a show of confidence navigated the bobbing craft to the middle of the harbor. It was blissfully quiet. Any of the fisher-men who still used the old harbor had returned hours ago, giving them the entire area to them-selves.

James pulled out a fishing line, stashed be-neath one of the seats and pulled Molly's basket out to tear off a piece of ham.

"Coming about," she said over the laughing and jokes of the boys. "Put that back, your Ma is going to scalp us," said Molly, "if she finds out you used good ham for bait."

"She doesn't have to know," said James pull-ing a large piece off and stuffing most of it into his mouth. "Ohhh," he said, trying to talk around a mouthful of ham, "What have we here?" Mark and Joseph tried to elbow each other out of the way for a better look. "Guess you must have for-gotten these three cookies kinda' squished down here."

Molly wasn't quite sure what happened next, but she thought she remembered Joseph grabbing for the basket, pushing Mack out of the way. She had let go of the tiller, a gust came out of the north. James grabbed the boom as it swung over, sweeping across the little boat. Mack had been standing and was the one knocked overboard. One of the boys lunged for him and the boat, unbalanced, heeled over sharply. For just a second, Molly thought it was going to right itself and went to reach for the tiller.

It was too late.

The unsteady craft capsized, its crew dumped into the chilly waters. Molly had never been much of a swimmer but kicked her feet hard to propel herself back to the surface. Her head bobbed up as she struggled to stay afloat. The mast, its sail lying on top of the water like a great gray sheet, flopped up and down with the waves.

"Where's James," yelled Joseph, shaking the water from his head.

"I'm right here," he said. They could hear him, but not see past the side of the hull that jutted up from the water. It looked like the belly of a giant dead seagull.

"Mack," the two boys yelled together

"Oh no," said Molly, "he can't swim." Not a stroke. He had never liked the water, but only went along to avoid the teasing. "Mack," she yelled, her eyes searching each wave as it lapped gently over the top of the icy water. If only Jack were here, she thought.

"Mack," they all yelled again, looking about. Molly tried to move around in the water, her shivering arms reaching in different directions. For just a moment she thought she saw what could have been a mop of dark blonde hair floating away. It wasn't. It was the bottom of her up-turned basket bobbing on the surface.

The two boys swam around the boat. James dove under the boat and Joseph strained and pushed and tried to right the boat but the weight of the drenched sail made it impossible. The sun was sinking in the sky, a few seagulls cawed overhead sounding a warning.

Molly pulled herself around the boat, feeling beneath it with her feet, running her hands along the gunnel. She looked up, a dinghy, powerful arms rowing, was bearing down on them.

It was Jim Bone, the Indian.

"Mack," she said, "We can't find Mack." Her voice was screechy, she wasn't sure if he'd understood. His eyes were everywhere. Had he heard her? His oars dipped into the water, again and again as he rowed hard, circling the hull jutting out of the water. Then he put his oars deep in the water, stopping any motion, he listened intently, watching every ripple in the water. He shook his head. It said no.

Holding the boat steady, he pulled her up out of the water. Tears and salt water mixed together. Within minutes he had hauled in the two boys, both quiet for once, and both shivering uncontrollably.

There were pockets of air trapped under the sail, and surely parts of the hull where he could hang on. Molly squinted into the fading light trying to see.

"Wait. Wait," she said. "Look, under the sail. There he is." Her hand was on the gunnel, ready to jump back in. Jim grabbed her arm and pulled her back. His oars dug deep into the frigid waters. It brought them around to the sail. It was floating like a tired grey rag on top of the gentle waves. He too saw the bump in the middle of the canvas. Reaching down he lifted the sail with his long powerful arm. Mack, tangled in the ropes, his face just above the water was blue. Molly could not recall how but in an instant, Jim Bone had him in the boat, lying across his lap. He banged on his back, trying to force out the trapped water. Nothing happened. There was no movement. Jim Bone stood in the tippy boat and holding him upside down, his hands tight on his ankles; he shook him and banged on his back all at once.

Mack was the color of an angry sky before a summer storm, but then he coughed. It shook his whole body. Water poured out of his mouth, and even his nose. His eyelids fluttered and he took a strangled breath. Molly gathered him up on her lap and rocked him gently, much as a mother would with a frightened child.

~

~ CHAPTER SIX ~

Molly stood over the table, cutting small carrots into smaller pieces and slicing the hard potatoes to slivers – there appeared to be more if the pieces were cut small. The stew pot was bubbling. The lamb bone and the handful of herbs had been simmering for most of the afternoon; it brought a not unpleasant aroma to the dank room.

The pot was suspended over the fire. The tug, mixed with a few twigs, would crack and snap now and again, shooting out bright little sparks. She leaned over the pot, trying to keep half an eye out for the whereabouts of Widow Grady. She'd been surprised more than once with a slap or a smack across her back with a fire poker or with the belt when the Widow wasn't pleased with something. The belt was kept close by as she used it often to threaten her sons. They all knew it was an idle threat, as she would rarely use it on her own flesh and blood.

It had been well over a year since Mack had nearly drowned. The Widow still held Molly responsible saying she should have known better than to take the boys out on the boat, and she certainly had never forgiven Molly for the loss of the ham.

"Get that corn bread mixed up or we're never going to eat," she said as she adjusted her body to a more comfortable position in her chair. It creaked in protest. Molly pulled the big wood bowl towards her and carefully measured the three cups of cornmeal, then shook the canvas sack for the remaining crumbs. This might be the last they'd be seeing of cornbread for a while. Adding a cup of flour, a pinch of salt, a teaspoon of sugar and three eggs was all it needed. Using the long handled wooden spoon she stirred until it was well blended and then poured it into the three-legged kettle. Heavy as it was, she lifted it to the hearth.

"Girl, now look, you've slopped it all over the sides. Can you not even do that right? Put that cover on, and give that stew another stir before it burns to a crisp." The Widow rarely found anything to approve of. Her mood was often grouchy, no doubt as she often felt so unwell.

Molly reached into the hearth, her arms not quite long enough to remove the cover from the simmering kettle. She turned to retrieve the hook to pull the suspended pot closer to her. Her light wool skirt brushed up against the coals as she turned.

The flames caught quickly.

Tired as she was, she didn't notice at first, then, feeling hot flames against her legs, she looked down. A scream filled the room. It was a terrified high-pitched scream. Using her hands she tried to beat out the flames that were rapidly traveling up the wool skirt. The Widow jumped up.

"Now look what you've gone and done," she yelled after the girl, who was wildly racing for the door. Widow Grady picked up the bucket of water and threw it at the flaming skirt.

"Stop running, you foolish thing," she commanded. But Molly screamed all the louder, the pain of the burned flesh on her legs making her feel faint.

"Lie down," yelled the Widow as she rushed at her, the quilt dragging behind her. "Lie down!" But Molly, frightened out of her wits, and trying to run from the pain ran out the door and down the path, the smoke and flames shooting out from behind her.Jack, his arms loaded with blocks of tug, heard the screams. Dropping his load he ran towards the house. Molly, her skirt blazing, terror in her eyes, arms outstretched ran towards him. He easily caught her and tackled her to the ground. Rolling her in the damp grass and slapping at the flames, he extinguished the fire, ignoring the flesh that was burning on his own hands.

It had taken only moments to crush the flames but the damage had been done. Her skirt hung in charred ribbons, her legs were raw and charred and blistered. Molly groaned in pain, her hands trying to reach out to touch what hurt so badly, but they would not obey her commands. She gritted her teeth. Tears streaked her cheeks. Her eyes glazed over and she sank into uncon-sciousness.

It was as if she were somewhere else listen-ing in on someone else's conversation. She heard Jack fading in and out. He sounded worried. She tried to pull herself out of her sleepiness, but every time she thought she was close, the pain in her legs forced her back into unconsciousness.

She thought she heard Madam Kaposhkin and could even imagine that she saw the wrinkled dark face leaning over her. She imagined she could even smell the burning tobacco from the ever-present pipe.

"She come with me. That be an end to it." Molly's eyes fluttered open. She knew not to move or she'd break open the flesh on her burned legs.

"She's not going anywhere, especially with you." It was the Widow Grady, her voice rising. "Why would she want to live with a gypsy woman on an old fishing scow?"

"I no gypsy and boat pulls in more cod than any other boat." She used her smoldering pipe for emphasis, pointing it at the fat woman in front of the hearth who was spilling out of the shabby chair.

"Well she's not going with you. She's needed here."

"Da," she said nearly spitting out the Russian "yes." "I see how she be needed here. Who else going to do work? Who else you going to beat on and belittle? How many weeks she been sick like this?"

Widow Grady started to rise from her chair, sputtering her denial.

"You hiding nothing. Everyone know. You not lay a hand on own sons but little Molly she be fair game. I seen the bruises. You no deny what I see."

"I never beat her," she spewed. "I may have cuffed her now and again but what young girl doesn't need an occasional slap?"

"There been too many of occasions is my thought."

"Well you can't have her and you can't prove a thing."

"She need to be in school, and need to not be stuck here every day waiting on all people. She come with me and that be an end."

"How dare you! How dare you enter my house and make these demands! Look what your husband did to my husband. He drowned him."

"You know that not true – your husband make my Stanley take him out. He know it not good weather. Your husband foolish."

The Widow sputtered and stammered and lost most of her words. She knew it was true but denial was easier. "He killed him."

Madam Kaposhkin, as if deaf, walked over to the bed where Molly was lying and scooped her up as if she weighed nothing. "You no Christian woman. Look at child, she very nearly dead," her words were garbled. Her pipe was clenched firmly between her teeth.

"I'm not the mother to this child. I took her in out of the kindness of my heart."

"That be good," she mumbled. "You not be her mother!"

"Well I know who she was..." She started with a conspirator's whisper.

"Da, but I think not. You stop your talk. I go now." Madam Kaposhkin held the too thin girl as if trying to share the warmth and the strength from her own sturdy body, "Open door now before I not be so nice anymore and get the law after you."

Widow Grady rose stiffly and waddling, crossed the room and pulled open the creaky door. She could not believe she was taking orders from the old fisherwoman.

"Hope you care for own sons more better then you care for this poor girl."

Molly unable to even raise her head felt

Madam Kaposhkin gently lay her down in the back of a wagon. She felt the boards creak in protest as the old fisherwoman hoisted herself up to the seat. "Go horse," she said to the old mule flicking the reins. He flicked his tail ignoring the command. "Can get boat through worst weather on this earth, have no way with stubborn animals." She continued to slap the reins on the old sway back, but he continued to swish his tail with his hooves rooted to the earth.

Jack, rounding the corner of the house, saw her plight and in three strides was at her side. Grabbing the bridle of the stubborn animal, he yanked hard and pulled him down the path. The animal quickly knew who was in control and that it was going to be easier to obey. In no particular rush, he trotted off, his hooves making squishy noises in the mud. Jack easily kept up with them. "I want to come with you," he said. "I can help."

"Nyet," said the old woman, reverting to her ancient Russian. "You gonna be needed here." She flicked the reins again.

Jack knew there would be little sense in arguing with the angered woman and left them with a halfhearted wave.

A great sigh escaped before Molly could stop it.

"You life good back there, Molly Anne?" asked the ancient woman as she continued to slap the reins on the mule's rump. "Jack came to my boat, he tell me things not so good."

"I'm fine," Molly whispered, trying hard not to move.

"That old baggage call me gypsy. I not like being called gypsy. Who she to call me gypsy?"

"Mmmm," said Molly trying to keep her legs perfectly still as they bounced down the road.

"I no damn gypsy woman," she said, stabbing angrily at the air with her pipe. "I be good Russian woman." As always her r's went on almost forever, pronouncing it more like Rrrrrrussian. "My husband was a Rrrrrrrussian Cossack. Nobody understand me when first I come here years ago so they call us gypsy. Imagine, me a gypsy. They jealous cause I be best damn fisherman on Godforsaken little island. What you think of that?"

She turned to look down at her charge who was trying desperately not to cry out from the pain in her legs. "Sorry Molly Anne, we be close, we almost there, child. You hold on, Doc's gonna fix you up, you wait, you see."

~

"Here, Doc. Told you I bring her."

"What do I want with a young girl?" he asked barely able to contain his annoyance.

"You make her well. She cook and clean for you. Widow Grady she got her all trained for you. You just fix her legs."

"I can't fix her legs. There's nothing that I can do. It's probably too late." He rubbed at his baldhead; his annoyance with the interruption was obvious.

"Told you," she answered laying her burden down on the bed. It was unmade and shoved against the wall. "Legs burned bad. She need good doctoring."

"Well I can't help her," he said. His voice had a sharp edge. There was no doubt the subject was closed. "Go find someone else."

"Doctor," she said, "You all we got. Way I sees it you been back a long time now, people try to leave you be, let you recuperate, let you get well. All I see is you hole up in house and not come to answer door when a body comes to call.

Now you got first patient. We see what you do with her. Good day," she said as she let herself out, not quite slamming the door behind her.

Molly lay on the bed wide-eyed at the conversation that had just taken place, but too infirm to object or even respond. The Doctor, as Madam Kaposhkin had called him, paid no attention to her and instead sat down heavily at the table. He poured himself a drink of amber liquid, spilling some that only added to the drips on the tabletop. She watched for a while as he continued drinking. His baldhead reflected the light from the fire. His shaggy brown beard had drops of liquid in it, catching the firelight. His eyes were hooded, showing little emotion. His body slumped in the chair, as his head came to rest on the good arm that was stretched out on the table. His other arm, with the sleeve empty below the elbow, hung at his side like a tired flag waiting for a breath of wind.

Night was falling. The room darkened, lit only by the dying glow of embers. Molly's eyes closed. They would no longer stay open. The tiredness and pain swept over her and she slept. Twice during the night she cried out in fear or in pain, but no one heard her. The man slept soundly, his head on the table, a thin line of drool seeped out from between his lips. It caught in the straggly, frayed ends of a beard that had been left untended for too long. The silence seeped into each nook and cranny. An eerie hush engulfed the darkened room.

~

~ CHAPTER SEVEN ~

"Girl, wake up. What're you doing here?"

Molly's eyes flew open. She tried to focus on the angry man staring down at her. He was leaning over her, shaking her shoulder. "What are you doing here?" he asked again, his steel blue eyes bored into her, his bald head was shiny in the morning light and his shaggy beard was wild, flying in all directions.

"Sir," she said, barely able to find her voice, "Madam Kaposhkin left me here. She said you'd fix my legs." The pain etched around her deep blue eyes was hard to ignore.

"Girl, you need a Doctor, and I'm not a Doctor." He wiped the back of his hand across his mouth, crumbs dropping from his beard.

Molly, frightened, pushed back the blanket

and tried to rise. The pain in her legs was both throbbing and stinging. It wouldn't let her rise and she fell back on the pillow, a barely audible whimper escaping from her lips.

"Girl, you can't stay here. I don't want you here. What the devil was that old baggage thinking? I can't treat you. Can't you see that? Get up and get out of here." But his cries fell on deaf ears. Molly could understand nothing. Her eyes were closed, her flushed cheeks sunken, her lips parted just enough to allow the sucking in of a few shallow breaths of air.

~

Much later, she woke. Silence filled the room except for the occasional snap of a wet twig meeting the flicker of a flame that refused to die. The candle had long ago burned itself out. She was quickly aware of the thick bandages wrapped tightly around her legs. The pain from the burns, still intense, had nevertheless lessened. She glanced over at the man with the shaggy beard, his good hand rubbing at his baldhead.

"Sir, may I have some water please?" There was no indication that he had heard her. She said it again only this time louder and then watched as he opened his eyes and tried to shake the sleep out of his head.

"What?"

"Sir," she said again, "if I might have some water." He turned in her direction, his eyes boring into her. Saying nothing, he rose from his place, his chair scraping across the wood floor as it was forcibly pushed back. Reaching into the water bucket he filled the dipper, leaving a trail of drips as he crossed the room.

"Here," he said holding the metal dipper out to her. She noticed the fine, long thin fingers but tried to look away when he brought his other arm around to balance the dipper.

"It's alright girl, it won't bite. I lost it in Gettysburg."

"I'm sorry Sir," she said, not quite sure what exactly he meant.

"The war," he said, his voice raspy as though from disuse. "They made me go. Pulled me right out of school, said they needed doctors desperately. They didn't care that I hadn't been in school long enough to be a doctor or how much I knew." A disgusted sort of snicker escaped as he looked away.

"Learned more about doctoring in those two years then I'd ever learned in a classroom. Here drink up now," he said holding the dipper to her lips. She drank with her eyes closed so she wouldn't have to look at the stump where there had once been an arm."It's alright," he said taking the dipper away, "If it hadn't been for the infection it would've just been a minor wound. Interesting what can happen without the proper medicine." He held his stump up and looked at it, revulsion clouding his eyes, "...was going to be a surgeon in Boston. Now look at this." He shook his arm and then turned away returning to his seat at the table. Reaching for the bottle and lifting it high he guzzled another long drink. Slowly his chin sagged to his chest.

~

She dozed, for how long she had no idea, but woke to the not unpleasant smell of soup simmering on the stove. A stove she thought, her Grams and Pap had one. She remembered how it had made cooking so much easier for Grams, not like the fireplace cooking that she been forced to do at the Widow Grady's. The doctor ladled out the hot soup.

"Drink it," he said as he passed the steaming bowl to her. His command just bordered on rudeness. She took it gratefully, her hands shaky, her stomach growling loudly.

"Thank you Sir," she said before spooning in the hot liquid. It burned her tongue.

"Careful there," he said, "Slow down, there's more where that came from. What's your name?" he asked, looking more closely at her. "You do remind me of someone."

"Name's Molly Anne," she answered while blowing on her soup, "but people just call me Molly."

"Who're your people?" he asked, staring down at her curiously. His voice was deep and though he didn't know it there was a soothing quality to it.

"Don't know Sir," she said, "I belonged to Grams and Pap, but they're gone."

"So you're not one of the Grady brood?"

"No Sir, they're all boys."

This brought a half smile to his lips. "Well that's what I thought," he said, not unkindly. "Drink your soup now," he said, "It's from Madam Kaposhkin. She, for some reason, thinks we need each other. You can stay," he said turning away, "until your legs heal, then we'll have to find a place for you." But his voice went unheard. Molly had fallen back on the pillow and was sound asleep, her curling blond hair spread in disarray, her dark lashes fluttered in sleep on pale cheeks. The bowl of soup forgotten.

~

~ CHAPTER EIGHT ~

"I'm coming, I'm coming," she said tossing back her long braids. At sixteen Molly Anne was tall and straight; she walked smoothly across the room with no sign of the limp that had plagued her those first few months after the accident. Her legs had healed. The Doctor's salves had done their magic. There were still scars and probably always would be, but few would know of themw. Chances were that they would not be seen under her long skirt. Most people would not remember what had happened and few would see the wounds. It was best to put it behind her. There was no one to blame. The fault was hers.

Sometimes she thought back to how the Doc had so reluctantly cleaned and bandaged and tended to her. He had told her later that he preferred that to the verbal lashing Madam Kaposhkin dealt out whenever she felt Molly was not receiving the very best of care. The Doctor had actually stopped most of his drinking while he tended his patient, but had quickly resumed his nocturnal habit once she was on her feet again. It had been his plan to make her well and then send her on her way, but somehow he had never quite gotten around to finding another place for her to stay.

The desperate knocking continued. "I'm coming," she said again, picking up her pace while smoothing back the escaping curls that framed her face.

Before she could open the door it was pushed open. "Molly, come quick." It was Jack, "Get the bag, bring the Doc, it's Ma." Molly could see the fright in his eyes. Without a word she turned and hurried to the main room.

"Sir," she said, "Sir, wake up," she shook his shoulder. "Sir, you're needed. We've got to go," she said, never having used any other title but "Sir."

He roused himself, shaking his head, squinting over at her. He still was not accustomed to her interruptions of his sleep. "What?" he asked, looking around, "what now?" his voice grumpy with sleep. He rubbed at his eyes.

"Sir, it's the Widow Grady, there's a problem and we need to go quickly."

"Alright, alright girl, for heaven's sake will you ever let me sleep in peace?" She ignored him as she always did and pulled his heavy cape down from the peg. She held it for him and was reminded again how much she didn't like the ragged cape with the scratchy wool. He'd brought it back with him from the War. He could certainly afford better but for reasons only he knew, he was adamant about keeping it. She watched as he settled it on his shoulders, pulling it closely around him, the length nearly dragged on the floor. Shabby and threadbare as it was, it offered little protection from the elements. Molly had tried to throw it out but he had clung to it and now looking at his tall frame nearly lost in the yards and yards of fabric, it was hard to tell if it was embracing him or protecting him or swallowing him up.

Pulling off her apron, she threw on her cloak and picked up the black bag. "Come along," she said almost as if she were speaking to a child.

Jack was standing by the door shifting from

one foot to the other, trying not to show his impatience. "She woke up bad," he said simply. All three climbed up onto the shay that Jack had brought around from the barn. The Doc took the reins. Jack sat on the back, his long legs trailed behind with the toes of his boots just touching the dirt road. The Doc flicked the reins again trying to get more speed from the aging mare.

It took little time to get over to the Grady's. Ginger, the gentle old horse, had little opinion on which way to go and would trot off in whatever direction that she was guided. The Doctor had, as usual, insisted on driving the creaky old wagon. There were enough things already that had been taken out of his hands. Molly knew to let him at least have control over that.

"Over there," said Molly.

"I know, I know," he said, irritation showed in his eyes and in his voice and the slap of the reins. The horse stopped on her own at the front walk. Jack, trying not to seem too impatient, had jumped off and stood holding the gate open. It was attached with only one rickety hinge. The Doctor picked up his black bag refusing to let Molly carry it.

"Where is she," he asked rubbing at his head.

Using his arm that ended in a stump, he patted down the two or three wisps of hair that refused to give up. He'd never reconciled himself to the fact that he no longer had a bushy head of hair. He'd lost it all while he'd been hospitalized during the war. Poor nutrition, the camp doctors told him, but it was as if all the roots to what had once been a fine head of hair, had been killed off - along with part of him, was Molly's thought. None of it ever grew back.

"This way," said Jack. The Widow Grady with her great bulk was stretched out on the day bed near the hearth. Molly could see that she was in serious distress. Her skin was a pasty grey white. There were beads of perspiration sprinkled across her forehead and upper lip. Her eyes were shut and one side of her face seemed to be drooping.

"Might be apoplexy," said the Doctor with little emotion. He picked up one of her great arms that was stiff and unresponsive, then took out his stethoscope and listened intently to her chest.

"What's apoplexy?" asked Jack.

"She's paralyzed on one side. It's something that happens now and again, something in the brain misfires." He tried to temper his remarks but kindness didn't come easily to him. He looked around at the three other pairs of dark brown eyes staring at him. "She's going to need care from now on. You may need to get help."

"I can do it," said Jack, "We don't need help. My brothers'll be help enough."

"Here then," he said, "I can give you some medicine to make her more comfortable, but she may not get much better."

Jack stuck out his chin and raised his head, "We'll care for her. She's our Mother." Molly's eyes looked around at the clutter and dirt and wondered just how four boys would be able to care for a house and meals and a sick and cantankerous old woman. The Doctor continued to examine her and then tried to make her comfortable, asking for a pillow and propping it behind her head.

Molly wandered around the room straightening this and that. She swept the hearth and hung the boy's jackets on the odd shaped nails pounded haphazardly next to the door. She lined up four pairs of boots - all too familiar, she thought. It had been well over a year since she'd been back in the house. Not much had changed, she decided, except without her there to do the cooking and cleaning everything had fallen into disarray. The table was thick with sticky goo and the windows were so encrusted with grime that little light was allowed to shine through. The room had the same dark shadows that she remembered.

"Molly are you coming?" asked the Doc with the final snap of his bag.

"I'll come along later," she said, "I just want to stay a bit to see that everything's set to rights."

"Humph," he said, shrugging his cape back on. Without even a by your leave, he unlatched the door and let it slam behind him. Jack went out to assist with the horse but returned almost immediately. He muttered something and shook his head, but whatever had happened, he let it go and came over to Molly.

"You don't need to do all this," he said trying to take the broom from her hands.

"I know," she said. "I'll just stay for a bit and tidy up some. I know where everything is, it won't take a moment, and then maybe I can come by once in awhile to see if there's anything I can help with."

"It's really not necessary," he said, and wrested the broom from her hands. He began sweeping in earnest. "You three go on upstairs and fix the loft. We've got to pull together now." There was an unmistakable take-charge tone in his voice.

"Do you have enough to eat?" asked Molly.

"Of course," he said. "I took over the garden when you left and I fish a few days each week, usually with one of the Jones brothers. Sometimes I help the Kaposhkin woman, but we're O.K. How about you, Molly? We've never stopped missing you," he shifted uncomfortably, moving the broom from one hand to the other. "The boys and I, I mean." She gave him a knowing look. They both knew his mother only missed having someone to tend to all the household chores.

"I'm fine. I help the Doc when he's called out and I have my own room." It was hard not to miss the sadness in her eyes.

"But do you like him?" he asked.

"Oh he's alright. It's his hand. He can't get used to it not being there.

"Well he shouldn't have gone and gotten it shot off."

Molly gave him a half smile, "It wasn't exactly shot off!"

"Did he tell you about it?"

"Yes he did." What she didn't mention was how he'd gotten so frustrated one night after he'd been drinking heavily. How he'd been trying to straighten bottles and pills and his doctoring tools and how in his clumsiness the entire bag had spilled onto the hearth, some of the bottles with their precious liquid smashing into a million pieces, their valuable contents gone forever. His irritation was such that he'd railed against everything, God and man alike. In utter frustration, he'd kicked out at the brick surrounding the fireplace, splitting open the toe of his leather boot.

Molly had been frightened beyond reason, his anger spilling over as he crashed chairs and dumped what was left in his bag, finally throwing it into the fireplace. When he'd destroyed nearly everything around him and his anger was spent, he stormed out the door down to the beach. Hiding in the corner, hoping she was concealed, she was so concerned over what he'd do next, that she followed him out. Her footsteps were silent. He staggered down to the shore where she saw him pacing back and forth; his heavy boots staying just above the tidal line, the cracked open toe making flip-flop sounds.

He'd be fine she thought. He needs time alone to work out his anger and frustration. Returning to the house, she cleaned up the mess. Hardly able to withhold the tears, she retrieved the slightly singed medical bag from the hearth. Why does he do this, she thought. Sweeping up the bits of glass, she collected the broken pieces of the two splintered chairs. They could be repaired later.

It hadn't been more than an hour when he returned. He was contrite. It took a while but he had talked to her. It was the first time he'd ever spoken to her other then to just give orders.

"He told me," she said turning back to Jack, "that his wound had been simple enough. He said a knife had gone through the palm of his hand. This was after they'd found out he was alive."

"He'd been on the battlefield and I guess they thought he was dead. They were dragging him to the morgue when someone discovered he was still breathing. Then they found out he had been in medical school before being conscripted into the army." She pushed back the curls that were straying from her loosely braided hair.

"After they'd bandaged his head and gotten him food they put him to work. He was trying to help all the injured soldiers lying outside of the hospital tent. It was a Confederate soldier that he was working on. He said the man had a gut wound and wasn't going to make it no matter what he did, but the Doc wanted to make him comfortable at least. Well the soldier misunderstood and thought all the helpers were going to kill him. He had a knife concealed in his trousers. A nurse was trying to cut his shirt off to get to the wound. He pulled the knife out and lunged towards the nurse. The Doc said he tried to stop him and instead the knife went right through his hand." She let out a great sigh and tried to decide if she should continue.

"I don't think he's ever discussed this with anyone," she said. "Not sure if I should continue." Jack was quiet, not sure what to say, so she went on.

"He said he had tried to push the nurse away. The wound was clean enough, but they had no medicine. He said he did everything possible to keep it bound and covered, but they were working in so much filth." She paused for a moment afraid her voice was going to break. "Even with a bandaged hand he couldn't stop his doctoring. He said they wouldn't let him. By the end of the day his bandage was soaked with everyone else's blood. After about a week he said it was putrid. He said he lanced it, soaked it, he did everything possible. He wrapped it. He washed it. And then the red line started up his arm. He knew, but he still didn't want to give up. His arm swelled up to twice its size. He said it took five of their biggest men to hold him down when the surgeon took the arm." A great sigh escaped.

"Jack, I at least know this much, he'd be dead now if they didn't. He knows that and sometimes I'm quite sure he thinks he would be a lot better off if he were dead." Tears were caught in the corners of her eyes.

"I didn't know," said Jack, "we'd only heard that it'd been shot off at Gettysburg."

"He never told anyone," she said, "and he's never really talked to me since that night. He only speaks to me to tell me what needs being done. I try to read to him at night to keep him calm but I'm not sure if he enjoys that or not. He did tell me that once he very much enjoyed Shakespeare and I've tried to read some of that at night, but

I'm not quite sure he's listening." She sighed, "I enjoy reading even though I don't know all the words. But I'm happy to do it. My Grams and Pap always read to me when I was little. That, at least, I remember."

"Molly, who were Grams and Pap, and why did they adopt you?"

"Don't know, and they never did adopt me. Madam Kaposhkin says they were visiting on the mainland and saw me as a little baby and decided they had to have me," she said. "They'd just lost their own daughter and were so distraught that everyone thought it was the best thing in the world for them. Grams said they were crazy about me. Even said I reminded them so much of their own daughter when she was a baby."

"I never met them," said Jack, "just went to their funeral after they drowned. My Mom said you looked a lot like their daughter Charity when she was a baby. Not sure how it all went but my Mom said she was good friends with your Grams and Pap before my Pa died."

"What happened to your father Jack?" she asked as she put the broom back, her sweeping completed. "You never told me."

"Not quite sure. His body washed up on the beach one day after he'd been missing for a few days. No one has ever figured out what happened. Only that he'd been fishing with old man Kaposhkin and they never even found him. Mrs. K.," he said using his own shortened version of the old Russian woman's name, "found the pieces of the boat they'd been on."

"Your mother never cared much for her, did she? Do you suppose it had to do with that?"

"Yeah, I'm sure, but she never told me. Ma wasn't quite so ornery 'til after Pa was killed. She was much kinder before. Seems like something snapped after we lost Pa."

The house was unusually quiet. The three boys who were supposed to be tidying the loft had somehow snuck out with no one noticing. They didn't seem to care. They knew well enough that when they were hungry they'd be back.

"What do you remember of your Grams and Pap?"

"I can hardly remember them anymore, except I know I sat on Gram's lap a lot and I remember both of them reading to me and how much I missed them when I first came here to live with you. Not sure what they would have done with me if your Ma hadn't taken me in." She stopped almost in mid sentence. "Jack, I've got to go, it's nearly dark," she said, interrupting herself. "I didn't mean to stay so long. I've got to get back to get supper for the Doc."

"I'll walk you back, Molly."

"No, no. I'm fine, let's get something going for your supper. You'll have to feed your mother, I'm afraid, for a while anyway. This is the same thing that old man Baxter had when I first started making calls with the Doctor. You'll have her sitting up soon enough and then maybe she can start doing things again."

It took little time to collect bits and pieces of foodstuff most of which were heaped in a pile in a bucket. Adding a few carrots and potatoes to whatever was bubbling away in the kettle, would, with luck, satisfy the boys for a while. There was still a partially eaten loaf of bread at the back of the brick oven. Handing Jack the long handled spoon, she told him, "just stir this now and again. Wait 'til it's good and bubbly then you can serve it." Picking up the last bit of the chopped turnip and half an onion, she threw it in the kettle.

"I've got to run," she said, "I'm late," and she

disappeared out the door, her long green cape billowed out behind her. The scent of fresh soap hung in the air.

~

~ CHAPTER NINE ~

"Sir, I can take the reins. You look tired."

"No. Leave me be." He pulled the threadbare cloak more closely around him. "I know what I'm doing." He wrapped the reins around his stump, looping them around his elbow, a way he had devised of holding the leather straps while his other hand was busy either fidgeting with his bag or wiping away the mist that collected on his bare head.

"A fine baby," said Molly trying to keep herself awake in the early hours. It was just before dawn and the sky hadn't quite lightened. The Doc, without intending to was paying more attention to those in need. At first he ignored every request, but when Mrs. K. had brought her to him, he had tried to get back in to it, although reluctantly. Then at Molly's urging, he'd finally picked up his doctoring bag and now, although he hesitated he most often went when someone requested him.

"The baby was early, too small," he said, "lucky to be alive."

"Well that baby meant a lot to them, after losing the other two," she said as she passed a piece of still warm cake to him. Like many of his patients Mr. Wilson had packed up a bit of food for them for their journey back home. He'd been so thankful, he'd offered to drive them home himself.

"She doesn't carry well," he said, "some women are just like that, not much you can do."

"But you were able to save this one and they're so pleased. He looked fine, his color was good and his breathing seemed good." Mollie was sixteen and already she knew almost as much about doctoring as the doctor. She'd accompanied him on most trips and acted as his hands doing as he instructed her. She'd already assisted him at three deliveries of new babies. She'd worked right alongside him, through the good and the bad, no matter how gruesome the task was. Once she'd had to hold a limb for him as he amputated it. She'd helped to clean accidental gunshot wounds, she'd drained abscesses, she'd sat up with fevered children and she'd closed the eyes of the deceased. She found that she was good at doctoring and enjoyed it and looked forward to accompanying him on his house calls. If for no other reason, she was able to get out of the house. It was the Doc's house and certainly was big enough with a sitting room, a kitchen, an entire loft for her as well as outbuildings. Much

and more comfortable than the Grady's had been. But it was only where she lived. Somehow she never felt she quite belonged.

It was still dark. The moon had disappeared from the sky, if it had ever been there at all, thought Molly. She wasn't sure. The fog was pea soup thick. Way off in the distance they could hear the bell as it clanged. It sounded every three minutes from the lighthouse, trying to warn all the ships at sea. The eastern horizon was just beginning to lighten, as another day was about to begin.

The Doc would sometimes talk to her if they were alone on the long carriage rides to or from one of the patient's houses. She knew he did it only to stay awake. The old mare actually needed little guidance on the island. When they were headed home, she always found her own way back to the warm barn.

"Is your cloak warm enough," she asked. Her intention was to keep herself from dozing off more than keeping the Doc awake. He hesitated a moment, then answered that "yes," it was more than he needed.

"Do you not want a new one," she asked, not really caring if he answered or not.

"Don't need one," he answered. "This is more warmth than I need." For a while they creaked along in the old farm wagon, hearing different morning sounds typical of the shore. There was the crashing of the waves as the last storm petered out and the occasional early morning birdcall.

"Got it in Gettysburg," he said. Her eyes were closed, the swaying of the wagon doing its magic to lull her to sleep. She heard what he said and could only respond with "Oh."

"They thought I was dead. I was a foot soldier and had been hit in the head with a rifle butt during the battle. They wanted everyone to become a soldier." He seemed to be talking more to himself then to anyone else. "They had pulled me out of medical school, but like everyone else I was given a rifle and sent to fight."

He spoke mostly to himself, not caring if anyone heard. Her breathing slowed as she listened, not sure if she was eavesdropping on a conversation meant only for himself. But he continued. "It was at the end of a four day battle. I guess I was lying in a heap at the bottom of a ravine. I never did get comfortable holding a rifle, never mind shoot it – my job was to save lives not take them." A huge sigh of disgust escaped before he could stop it.

Wrapping the reins around his stump, he wiped at his nose with the fresh handkerchief. Each morning she'd slip one that was newly washed into his pocket, removing the one from the day before. He never commented on it or even noticed.

"They found me and assumed I was dead. The weather was so hot we nearly couldn't breathe. There were no litters to carry off the wounded or the dead so the burial team took this cape from someone else they had carried off and rolled me into it as a way to drag me off to the morgue."

Molly peeked between closed lids. He was

staring far off into the distance as if listening to something that only he could hear.

"If there hadn't been a way to drag me off the field that day chances are good I would never have made it. They would have left me." He took another swipe at his nose. "As it was they were quite sure I was dead – or would be soon. It was just one more body to be dragged off the field. Well some bright young grave digger unrolled me from that cape and discovered I was still breathing." He shifted uncomfortably in his seat. "This cape will be with me forever."

The old mare continued plodding forward. "Fog is thick," he said, breaking into her half slumber.

"Yes it is," she said, glad that Ginger knew her way, "We'd be in trouble if we had to walk in this." The drowsiness was leaving and she listening a moment. An odd stillness had enveloped them. Sitting up a little straighter, she stared into the swirling fog. Were those voices or just her imagination? She strained to hear as the distant sound of the all too familiar bell clanged again to warn the ships off the rocks. It was hard to tell about sounds in a deep fog. It all tended to be distorted and was often all around them, making it difficult to determine just which direction it was coming from.

"Humph," he said under his breath, his eyes becoming alert. So maybe he had heard it too she thought.

Pushing back the hood of her cape she listened more intently but the only sound she could hear was the rhythmic sound of the waves splashing into the rocks and washing along the shore. The far off sound of the fog bell seemed more distant.

The raindrops felt icy as they danced through the air. She felt her skin prickle with the cold as she pulled her sleeves down trying to cover her fingers.

"Maybe once the sun is up it'll clear and burn off the fog," he said. "Not gonna' warm up much today though, from what I can tell. More'n likely we've got a good month of cold still to go."

"Well," she said chattering idly, enjoying that he was actually carrying on a bit of a conversation. "It won't be long before I can put peas in. Widow Grady always said peas go in the first full moon in March and she always had a good ..." She froze suddenly, listening intently. She could hear Ginger's muffled clip clop over the sandy path and the crash of the waves as they smashed on the rocky shore; she even imagined she could hear herself breathe but there was something else.

"I did hear something," she whispered. He too sat up straighter, straining to listen. A distinct "Help" came from out of the fog, but from exactly where was hard to tell.

"Down on the beach," she said, her voice low as she strained to hear.

There were more distant voices, "Help us. Please help us."

He pulled hard on the wagon. "Hold horse," he said to the old nag. Before they had come to a complete stop Molly had jumped down off her high perch.

"I'll go," she said listening for just a moment to the horrible sound of wood grinding against granite boulders. "It's a ship up on the rocks. We'll need help."

"You can't go down there," he said. "You're just a girl. There's nothing you can do."

"And I suppose you can," she said angrily over her shoulder as she lifted her skirt to set off at a run.

"I'm coming," he answered jumping down after her.

Together they scrambled over the rocks be-tween the road and the beach, choosing their footing with care. Molly arrived first at the edge of the water. The sky was lightening in the east, casting just enough light for them to realize they could see almost nothing in the roiling fog.

"Help us. Help!" screamed voices out of the swirling mist.

"We have to get a boat," he said. "Whoever they are, we have no other way to save them."

"I'll go get help," she said turning back to the road. Ignoring the cold she hiked up her skirt and climbed back up over the rocks, her long legs giving her speed. Effortlessly she swung up to the high seat on the wagon. As she picked up Ginger's reins she turned back for a last look. The swirling fog cleared for just a moment, just long enough for her to see the Doctor remove a flagon from under his cape. He took a long pull on the contents. The fog silently crept back around him, swallowing him up, making him disappear into the morning mist as if he had never even been there.

Molly turned her attention back to the horse, slapping the reins harder than she meant to.

Why did he continue doing that? Usually he only drank at night, after the sun went down. That was when the demons seemed to come out of the walls to attack him, assaulting his memories. At night if he wasn't out treating someone, he spent hours in front of the fireplace staring into the flames, taking long swigs from his bottle. She would creep away to her loft; he had forgotten she had even been there.

Her room was kept comfortable by the bricks that absorbed the warmth of the fire from below. They held that heat through the long night. In winter, she kept her mattress snug up against the bricks, letting the warmth carry her through the night.

Often, long after she'd gone to bed, she'd hear him stumble to his room and fall on his bed. Rarely did he even bother to change into his nightshirt. If a knock came at the door for assistance on one of those nights, she knew she wouldn't be able to rouse him. Whoever it was would have to be turned away until morning. As much as she had learned from the Doctor it would never do to go out without him to tend to anyone. Many a night she had lain awake in the darkness listening to the piteous cries of nightmares that must have haunted him. It would send shivers up her back.

As the light of day stole in, most of the warmth in her room would be gone. Reluctant to leave the safe cocoon that she'd created in the down filled quilt, she'd force herself to get up.

Mornings were never easy. He would lurch through the rooms having little memory of the night before. His breakfast of a bowl of oatmeal and dried apples was always prepared and waiting for him. Then patiently Molly would pour cup after cup of steaming black coffee. Slowly he would get himself back together, always grumbling about this and that.

The memories kept pricking at her brain. "C'mon," she said to Ginger, "we've got to find help." She turned and looked back once more. She could just make out the lone figure on the beach. He had put the flask away and appeared to be yelling into the grey fog.

Ginger trotted off in an uncharacteristic fast gait bringing her to the nearest house. "Mr. Higgins, Mr. Higgins," she said pounding on the wood door. "Help, Mr. Higgins." It had taken her little time to arrive at the weathered shack. It was down by the water, but still close to town.

"Help, open the door." It was near time for most of the fishermen to be out, but with the fog and the blowing icy rain, they'd be taking their time. The door was pulled open.

"What is it?" The man held up a flickering lantern, his hair disheveled from sleep.

"There's a boat up on the rocks down by the Bluffs. We need help."

"Well, girl, you wait just a minute. Come in, why don't you, no sense standing out in the weather," he said as he pulled her in the door. Accustomed as they were to ships going aground and some even breaking up on their treacherous coast he showed no surprise. Their lighthouse saved many, of that they were sure, but still there were times in the fog when even the best ship's captain could become confused.

"Let me get my rain gear, and I'll be out. Whyn't you go on down and get the others," he said squinting at her in the low light. "Think most should be about. I'll go on up and get Jack Grady. He'll help out."

Together they left the house, he heading up the hill to find Jack, and she jumped back up on the wagon to head down to the dock to find the others.

They took off at a near gallop, Molly surprised at the pace that Ginger could go. Arriving in town she guided the old horse down to the docks.

She could see Madam Kaposhkin's candle glowing through the porthole as the grey fog swirled through the air. Molly knew she would come. Maybe together they could find some of the others. Bits of iciness blew about, settling on her cape, making her shiver.

"Whoa," she said to old Ginger as she threw the reins down. It startled a group of seagulls standing sentinel at the edge of the dock. They ruffled their feathers and eyed her suspiciously as they craned their necks to see what the intrusion was all about.

Feeling the sting of the sleet she pulled her cape more closely around her as she rushed down the splintery pier, nearly colliding with the Jones brothers and Mr. McGill. They had been standing next to the boats, their collars pulled up and their woolen caps pulled low, undecided as to whether or not it would be worth their while to head out on such a foul day.

"Ship up on the rocks," she said, "down by the Bluffs," she pointed in the direction, as if they didn't know.

"I'll get a wagon," said Mr. McGill as all three jumped into action. Their boots made heavy clunking noises as they stomped up the gangway.

Molly stopped on the pier next to the "*Resolve*" calling out "Hello the boat."

Madam Kaposhkin appeared almost instantly. "Da?" she said, slipping into her native Russian, her pipe smoldering between her lips. "What is it you need?" Molly looked down at her and for a moment and wondered how this old woman could stay warm through the winter on one small boat.

"Boat up on the rocks."

"Ah," she said, "A moment please. I will get my wrap and we be off." It took only minutes for them to get settled in the wagon.

"Dastardly day. Is no surprise with a wreck. We go, we help," she said, patting Molly's hand.

~

~ CHAPTER TEN ~

The rain had turned to icy droplets blowing through the fog. They spurred Ginger on to go faster in her race to get to the other side of the island. The old mare easily found her way along the familiar bumpy road. Conversation was nearly impossible with the crashing of the waves and clattering of the horse's hooves and Molly's repeated demands of "Go Horse." Madam Kaposhkin seemed content to chew on the stem of her unlit pipe.

The sky had lightened considerably as they pulled up to the beach. They were surprised to see some of the islanders already gathered. Her eyes tried to see into the fog to find the Doctor, but he was nowhere to be seen. But even through the swirling fog, it was easy to see how the beach was littered with debris that had washed up from the wreck; it must have broken up quickly.

"Ah, a ship bound for New Bedford," said the old woman, "Bound for the mills." It was hard to mistake the bales of cotton floating in with the incoming tide.

"Probably from Charleston or Savannah," said Molly. "Surely not familiar with our waters."

Molly searched the fog. There were only a handful of islanders, but the rest would be there soon enough. She saw three bodies lined up in the sand, two face down. She caught Mr. McGill's eye as he shook his head as if to say they're gone. The mist came in waves, sometimes blotting out nearly everything and other times thinning just enough so she could see the islanders gathering on the edge of the water. Bill Jones had cupped his hands and was yelling into the grey mist, "Hello out there."

There was a distant weak answer, one voice, maybe more saying, "help us."

"They're coming," yelled the elder of the Jones brothers as he cupped his hands around his mouth, trying to form a megaphone. "Hang on."

"And where would be the boat from town?"

asked Madam Kaposhkin standing at her elbow. "Ach, the fog," she said answering her own question. "Not too much that can be done."

"There's got to be something. We can't just leave them out there," said Molly, "Isn't there someway that we can help?"

"Da, we take that old skiff of Sam Brown's. We row out, maybe we be fools in this fog. Might miss 'em. End up in middle of Atlantic." Her thick grey eyebrows rose as if questioning Molly.

"'Perhaps we should try," said Molly. "If those men are in the water, they're not going to survive much longer."

"Da," she said, "We two go. Won't hold more. Need to leave room in boat if there be others."

"That boat will hold at least two more if we can find anyone."

"True enough, we try."

It took only a few steps for the two to be swallowed up by the fog. One was old and stooped and the other young and sprightly with a step that tried to slow its pace to allow the old one to keep up. Together they made their way down the beach to Sam's place. Their boots made crunching noises as they tramped over the shells and stones littering the beach. The old Russian worked hard at keeping up with Molly's long legs but was easily winded. She was a boat person not a landlubber, she reminded Molly as she hobbled along, struggling to keep pace.

The fog was treacherous and confusing but they recognized the wooden pathway that extended down to the beach that they knew to be Sam's. There were still a few boards left that marked the pathway to his shack. Those were the few that had survived the spring tides and winter storms and hadn't been torn up and flung far out to sea. He owned or had rights to a wide expanse of beach. He made his living by "farming" his stretch of the rock strewn shore. It just washed right up to his door. His farming mostly consisted of collecting the Irish moss clinging to the rocks or tossed up after a storm. It was what Molly had done for the Widow Grady. It seemed so long ago. But his other pastime was collecting the flotsam and jetsam that washed up after a storm. He'd found such treasures as wooden chairs and dinghies and sometimes an unexpected bundle of tea from China or even a crate of pigs that had been washed overboard.

Sam was a hermit, staying to himself most of the time in a humble but tidy little fishing shack where he'd lived for most of his life. It appeared that he'd already been down to the beach as parts were already picked clean of the moss. She had met him just once when he'd come to the Doctor for a badly infected hand. He'd caught it with a fish hook and had attempted to cut out the hard piece of offending metal but the curved and sharp barb on the end held it tight and over a few days he'd dug and pulled and tried everything but nothing would get that hook out of the fleshy part of his hand. As he worked on it, it became more and more infected. His visit with the Doctor was brief.

After draining the abscess and having Molly wind a long bandage around it, the Doc rolled back his own sleeve. "You want this?" He shook his stub in the dumbfounded hermit's face. "Well, this is what you're going to be left with if you don't take care of that infection." The hermit stared wide-eyed at what was left of the Doc's exposed arm. It seemed that everyone in town knew about the missing hand except the Hermit.

Molly remembered how she was pressed into service to hold his arm steady and to keep the pan under it as it was lanced and drained. She had held tight wanting very much to retch, but she was kept so busy she quickly forgot how her stomach was doing somersaults. The wound was quickly bandaged under the Doctor's watchful eye after it'd been cleaned. Most of the bandaging of the wounds was now her responsibility, as she was very dexterous with her long fingers; and, of course, two hands worked better than one.

The Doctor had warned the hermit that if he didn't keep it scrupulously clean he'd end up like him. "In fact come back in two days," he'd said, "I'll look at it again." Of course the hermit never did and as far as Molly knew his hand had healed.

"Molly," said the Russian lady pulling her back to the fog-enshrouded beach, "there is skiff. Ah, and he left oars," she said, "a good man that hermit." Neither bothered to go and tell the owner they'd return it. He knew. If he found it missing, whoever had need of it would most certainly return it. There was little theft on the island. Molly pushed while Madam Kaposhkin dragged the front line pulling the little boat down to the water.

"Go Mrs. K.," she said using Jack's shortened version of the old woman's name, "hop in, I'll push us off." She hiked up her long skirt and tucked it up under her belt. No time to take her leather boots off. Wading into the freezing water, she pushed the boat off, jumping in as the water reached above her knees.

"Brrrr," she said, "don't think it gets much colder than this." Her companion sat heavily in the middle seat adjusting the oars, her pipe tucked deep in the canvas apron pocket. She pulled hard on the splintery poles. They creaked in the metal oarlocks.

"Molly, you listen. You tell me what you hear. Fog plays big tricks with sound. Don't want to miss and go out to ocean." The old lady dipped the oars deeply into the icy Atlantic, pulling hard, making them shoot forward. It took only three attempts to get them past the breakwater and out onto the ocean.

"Ha! I still best oarsman around," she said "Let others wait for town boat."

"It may not even come," added Molly.

"Water calmed some," said the old woman, "Quieter winds. What do you hear?"

Molly strained to listen as Madam Kaposhkin shipped the oars and sat intent on listening, her eyes darting back and forth through the churning fog. There was the lap of the water on the boat and the distant crash of the waves on the shore, but everything else seemed quiet. There were no voices, only their own. The fog swirled silently around them. Tiny drops of mist caught in Molly's hair. Droplets collected on her eyelashes and eyebrows as they sat in silence. The little boat rocked and bobbed about with a gentle motion. The sea had calmed almost as if it were being pressed down by the heaviness of the fog.

"I hear nothing," said the old fisherwoman. "We go look that way," she said pointing a gnarled finger. "Current does strange things." She again dipped the oars in the water and pulled on them with little effort, her arms strong from all her years on the water. "Molly, where was Doctor? You driving his wagon?"

Molly shifting uncomfortably on the hard wood seat said, "I left him on the beach while I went to get help. I have no idea where he's gone off to."

"And is it good that you live with him?"

"I'm fine."

"Is he good to you? I know you help him."

"We're fine; he's not too hard on me. He goes his own way. I help him with his doctoring, it's not hard, he tells me how to do it," she said, reaching for the baling bucket. The hermit hadn't spent any time keeping the old skiff properly caulked and water was seeping in along every seam.

"He better Doctor with you, I hear. He show you what to do. No?"

"He is a very good doctor, but he only does it if people push him. He doesn't really volunteer, and he shows me how to do things so I can help him."

"He skilled Doctor, you learn a lot. He learn to treat you better."

"Oh, I don't mind, he's good enough to me." Not meaning to be heard she said, "it's better than where I was.""Da," she said, "Molly, for long, long time I want to talk with you. Things I need to tell you." She leaned on the oars, no longer rowing, drops of seawater beaded up on her canvas apron. The fog was thick. The silence surrounded them. The old Russian stared at Molly. Indecision filled her eyes. Molly stared back, a question in her eyes.

"Da" said the ancient woman. "I tell you what you need to know."

~

~ CHAPTER ELEVEN ~

Again they dipped their oars into the frigid waters. There was little sound but they stopped after making a bit of headway to listen. There were no calls of help.

"Mrs. K. what is it you want to tell me," asked Molly. Her voice was hushed like the morning fog.

She paused and Molly wasn't sure if she heard her but was reluctant to ask again and then she spoke. "Molly, it is about you. It is about who you are." Madam Kaposhkin put the unlit pipe between her teeth then dipped the oars back in the water. Molly could hear her teeth grinding on the stem of her pipe, her discomfort with the conversation unmistakable.

What then?" she asked, her curiosity piqued.

"Help, help me," came a faint voice out of the fog.

"Over there," pointed Molly, "Quick."

Biting hard on her pipe, she dug the oars deeper into the frigid Atlantic and in a split second was once again forcing them forward.

"I see someone," said Molly. "We're coming," she yelled into the swirling grey air. "Hold on."

"I see him," said the old woman straining at the oars and squinting into the churning mist. They could make out a sailor, his arm flung across a large piece of debris, his head resting on his extended arm. There appeared to be another one close by, his arm clinging to an opened bale of cotton. The Russian, a determined look furrowing her brow, rowed hard to reach the two. As they pulled up next to them Molly reached out to help pull first one then the other on board, their arms so stiff with cold they were unable to help. The second sailor was not moving at all, his eyes shut as if in sleep. Together the two women hoisted and pulled and struggled to not capsize the boat. With many grunts and "we can do it," they were able to pull the bodies aboard. The first sailor looked up gratefully at the old woman's wrinkled face as they lowered him onto the floor of the dinghy. Molly pulled off her cape and tucked it protectively around the two shivering bodies.

"We bring them in, Molly. I don't hear others. This one close to dead," she said nodding towards the one that appeared to not be breathing. She pulled hard on the weathered oars. "Reminds me of day I find Mike Grady."

"You mean Jack's Dad?"

"Aye," she said. "That would be him." Either perspiration or droplets from the fog were dotting her upper lip and forehead, as she pulled harder on the oars. "Same day like this, fog like pea soup, very bitter cold. But that Grady fellow, he insist my Stanley go out with him to the mainland. Never again saw them alive." Molly reached down and shivering with cold she tucked her cape more securely around both of the shaking men.

"Is that why Widow Grady doesn't like you?" she asked.

"She have no reason not to like me. I be the one found her Mike Grady. Haul him in. Drowned for sure. Don't know why she think my Stanley responsible. But they never find him; only find parts of boat - my boat. It was Mike

Grady that make my Stanley go out that day. They both know weather coming in. Widow Grady start talk that it be my Stanley's idea to take boat out. That not the truth. I heard them arguing. My Stanley say no but Grady say he owes him."

"My husband never found. I find piece of wood from boat and Stanley's wool cap I knit myself. No reason I wouldn't know what was his. He dead and gone, but no one will believe old Russian fishing woman so let them doubt and let them talk"

"Was there a storm?"

"Da, but later. Ah, this island has much that isn't spoken about. I think maybe it been a whale. Storm was later. After they been missing for a day came storm. But those hump backs, they nothing but trouble if you don't stay out of their way. That day they were out there, I seen them myself."

One of the bedraggled sailors started to speak, his accent so thick he couldn't be understood. Mrs. K. became suddenly alert. She began babbling in a language that Molly had never heard.

"What are you saying?" she asked. Mrs. K.

reached down and pulled back the blanket covering the faces of the two bodies and again, spoke rapidly in her own language. The sailor blinked up at her, a half smile coming to his lips, blue from the cold. He was shivering but wanted to see who it was speaking to him. Molly understood only "Da, Da," when he agreed with something that Madam Kaposhkin said to him.

"What did he say," asked Molly. With a wide grin the Russian said "Why he from the homeland. I no hear this language in so long. He sound wonderful. From near my home. He know of my family."

The sailor, shivering so that he shook the boat, spoke again. Again Mrs. K. smiled. The sailor looked at her as though he was seeing an angel up close. "What then?" asked Molly.

"Ah, long story," she answered.

"But tell me then," said Molly. "We're a ways from the shore still."

"He know my family. They have much land still in Russia. He say some still living and are well known." She smiled a private smile.

"Tell me more," said Molly.

"Someday," she answered. "Not today. Here now, we're at shore already. You get set. Jump off and pull us in."

She didn't need to say even that as Molly was already standing with rope in hand ready to leap over the edge into the shallow water.

The men on shore quickly surrounded the little boat, pulling it up onto the sand, hands reaching in to help the nearly frozen sailors.

~

It was hours later when she made her way back home, allowing Ginger to find her own way. Letting the door slam behind her, she was too tired to care. She was not surprised to see the Doc in his usual place at the table staring into the glowing embers of what was left of the fire.

"Where were you?" she demanded facing him. "Men could have died. You could've helped. Must you always be drinking?"

"I wasn't drinking," he said. A vein in his temple throbbed.

"I saw you drinking. I saw you on the beach with the flask."

"It was coffee, I'll have you know. There are other things that come in a flask besides that demon rum, Molly. Mr. Winslow, for your information, poured it in when he came to help us."

"Why did you leave?" Unwanted tears clouded her vision.

"Molly, calm yourself. You need to slow down. You're tired. You don't know what you're saying."

"Yes I do." She stamped her foot, surprising herself with the depth of her anger. "How can you tend to people if you're always drunk?"

"I'm not always drunk."

"Yes you are and all these people are depending on you. You," she said again, "and all you do is feel sorry for yourself, and how your life is such a mess, and how your life could've been." He lowered his head into his one hand but she was not about to stop. "Life isn't always the way we want it to be. Sometimes we just have to make the best of what we've got." Tears of anger, frustration, embarrassment at having spoken out, started to roll down her cheeks. She had spewed it all out. After all, she thought, what did she have to lose? She didn't belong here anyway. In complete misery she turned and slammed back out of the door leaving him, cold and angry, his hand rubbing at the stump of his arm.

She spent that night in the barn, curled up

in the hay with only Ginger for company. She missed their nightly readings. It had become close to a passion for the Doctor to listen to her each evening. He had so many books, many with frayed and worn bindings; they'd been read so often. Some had notes in the margins but most notes were illegible, either smudged or water streaked. In *Evangeline,* a book by Longfellow someone had crossed out a name where it had said, "Where is my love now?" Another word had been written in, but it was blurred and hard to make out. It may have been Charity but she wasn't sure. An odd thing to do, she'd thought as she returned the book to its designated place.

He was not always keen on her reading his books unless she read aloud to him. There were a few books of poetry but he kept those at the bottom of his pile. Her favorites were *Robinson Crusoe* and *Gulliver's Travels.* They must have been his favorites too as he would sit quietly while she read. Most often, though, when she would look up from her reading to see why he was so still, his eyes would be staring off into the distance, focused on something only he could see. Sometimes she'd look up to find his head fallen forward onto his chest, his eyes closed in sleep.

For the next week she stayed close to the house avoiding him whenever she could. With the help of Mrs. K., he had patched up the sailors and sent them on their way, back to the mainland to pick up another ship. The excitement was over.

No sooner had the sailors been sent off than he was called out to attend to another injury. Molly stayed in her room. She did not go with him. The patient was the hermit! He had let his wound fester for weeks and by the time he decided it needed attention, the arm had to be amputated.

~

~ CHAPTER TWELVE ~

It's intolerable she thought. True he hadn't had anything to drink but cider or water since that day when the ship went up on the rocks. She'd been so angry with him that she'd avoided him whenever she could after she had given him the tongue-lashing she thought he deserved. But his brooding silences and dark glowering looks were more than she could endure.

Today, once again, he'd gone down to pace on the beach. She could just make out his lanky figure in the distance, always staying just out of reach of the waves; a lonely figure pacing back and forth. She watched as he rubbed at the stump of what had once been a whole arm, his oversized cape billowing out behind him.

"Well I don't care," she said out loud. "I don't

care how he feels or what's happened to him. I can't stay here one minute longer."

Where could she go? Back to Jack's? The Widow Grady had improved and was able to move around some. The boys had tried to help and Jack said it was working out. He said they were thankful that she wanted to help but it wasn't needed. They'd be fine.

Then where she thought? Certainly not any-where on the island. "I'll go to the mainland," she said firmly. "There's got to be work there." Sitting down at the table, she picked up the Doctor's writing pen and began: "Dear Sir." She chewed at the end of the pen, listening to the endless tick-tock of the clock as it marked the passing time, much like a heartbeat she thought. It re-minded her of Grams and Pap and how she wished she could remember more of her life with them. A damp blot formed on the paper, she swiped at it and then with great care dipped the pen in the ink and began. She wrote her thanks for allowing her to stay after he had cured her badly burned legs. She continued that it really was time for her to make her own way and find a place where she could belong. There was nothing else she could write. Carefully blotting the scrawled words, she folded the paper and slipped it into an envelope.

Feeling relieved and maybe a bit scared, she took the few possessions that she owned, including some of her favorite shells, and put them in a canvas bag and walked out the door. A puff of wind caught it and it slammed behind her. "Good bye forever," she said and made her way down the crushed oyster shell path. She would not look back.

The day was deceptively balmy for the end of March. The breeze was calm, not a cloud in the sky, the sun was beaming its pale yellow light from low in the eastern sky. She hoped she wasn't too late to find the *Resolve*. The fishing boats went out only sporadically during the changing weather of early spring. This day being so balmy could well be one of the days when Madam Kaposhkin would choose to sail off.

Hurrying down the path towards the waterfront, Molly clutched her canvas sack protectively to keep it from bursting open. She startled a group of seagulls standing sentinel, guarding the dock. They eyed her suspiciously. Standing with one leg tucked up as if keeping it in reserve, they waited patiently for the time when it would be needed. Their yellow feet with toes splayed open were in sharp contrast to the grey of the dock. Deciding that the intruder with the grey sack was too close, they rose as one. Their squawking disapproval cut through the silence of the morning. Their wings kept them aloft as they circled the waterfront in search of a safe place to land.

The *Resolve* was tied up in its usual spot. Molly stood, unsure. She stopped to watch the barnacles that were very much at home fastened to the pilings that supported the dock. They opened and closed almost in rhythm as they drew in the saltiness of the ocean, keeping time with the lapping water. A thin trail of smoke drifted out of the boat's stovepipe, blackened with age. It trailed off, going in no particular direction.

"Mrs. K.," said Molly standing on the pier. "Are you about?" It took a few moments only for the ancient lady to poke her head out of the cabin. The always present pipe was smoldering between her lips. There was delight in her eyes when she looked up at Molly.

"Come aboard," she said, her gnarled short-fingered hand shading her eyes. "You always welcome. How you be, child?" Extending a warm but work-worn hand she helped Molly on board.

"You come in, now," she said taking her arm and guiding her down into the cabin. "And here, sit, sit, sit. I get you fresh tea." A red and blue quilt was thrown across the bunk and a red and white tablecloth covered the round table dominating the middle of the small space. The four portholes were covered with yellow curtains, not quite as fresh as the day they were hung but nevertheless a cheery addition to the small cabin.

The old woman pushed the pile of sail canvas that she'd been busy with onto the floor. "Here Molly Anne, sit here, there be plenty of room." That always made Molly smile: the space was so small that the table was half extended over the bunk and there was room only for the small black stove and one stool.

"What is it, child?" she asked, "tell me what is the problem." She had never been one to put up with excess chatter. "There be trouble. Yes?" She leaned over to pull a taper out of the stove, relighting her pipe and inhaling deeply.

"Mrs. K," Molly said trying to look stern. "I thought the Doctor said you shouldn't be smoking anymore." There was a twinkle in her eye as she admonished the old woman.

"Ah bother child," she said, crinkling up her eyes and laughing. "Something got to kill me, pipe better than most things." She exhaled little puffs of smoke into the air as she leaned back on the bunk.

"Why you here today, and how you know I be here?" She patted Molly's hand. "I want to go to fish with good weather but I get busy fixing sail."

"I have to leave," she began abruptly. "You can help me. You're the only one of the islanders who will. You've said so many times if I ever need help just ask you. Well here I am, I need help now. I need to get away from here." Rushing breathlessly into the long story about the Doctor's continuing silence and disinterest, she told how he'd abandoned everyone at the wreck, leaving them all to tend to everything themselves."

Mrs. K. interrupted, "but he did patch up the sailors and got them off to the mainland."

"I know, I know, but he's always angry and has little interest in helping anyone. I need to get away. Maybe if I go to the mainland I can find out who my mother was or try to find my people."

"Ah I think not," she said as she puffed slowly on her pipe.

.   "And why not?" Molly asked, a tear slipped unnoticed down her cheek "Everyone else has family. I want to start again somewhere else, where I can belong. I want to go and have a real job. I can work. There are all sorts of things I can do. Help me, please Mrs. K. You're the only one who can."

"Molly Anne, what can I do child? I take you in here, but you see we can't even sit comfortable together. How we live together?"

"No. I want to go to the mainland. There's nothing here for me. He's so cruel and unfeeling. I need to get away from here."

"Molly Anne," she said as she patted her hand, "I need supplies, and need to visit old friend in Providence, it been far too long. I take you with me and you stay with her for awhile, just 'til you get bearings."

"Oh could I really?" she asked, her mood changing instantly. "That would be just wonderful, Mrs. K." In such close quarters, she didn't have to reach very far to give her protector a hug.

"Now dry tears. You and I have a nice chat on our way over. I've been meaning to..." she started, but then let her voice trail off.

"Now," she continued, "Life not so bad. Come out and hoist sail for me. Weather has cleared. We have tea when we underway."

It took no time at all to hoist the patched sail and head out into the beckoning day. It took even less time to sail out of the protection of the Island harbor. With a whole day ahead of them they tacked lazily back and forth, the wind coming in occasional light gusts. There would be more than enough time to get to the mainland. The gulls followed them in near silence as they floated along in the gentle breeze. Occasionally one of the grey and white birds of the sea screeched loudly at some unknown threat and then fell silent again.

Three hours had passed with the *Resolve* gaining very little headway in the light breeze. If she were on her own the Russian lady would have dropped the sail and pulled up and emptied the few scattered lobster pots that belonged to her and then dropped a line in over the side to pull in whatever was biting that day. The big nets that the larger boats used in catching fish were not for her. Her needs were small. Bringing her catch back to the dock she would keep only what she needed and would sell the few fish or the lobsters that she pulled in that day.

Today she would do neither. With a bit more breeze it would be an easy sail to the mainland with her young friend. Standing guard at the wheel she glanced over at the western horizon. "Uh oh," she said becoming instantly alert. Storm clouds appeared from nowhere and were rapidly piling up, one on top of the other, the grayness ominous. They hadn't been there earlier. Molly looked to the west, where the old woman was pointing. She had been around the water long enough to know there was trouble brewing.

"Not good," she said. Her eyes squinted up as they took in the blackness of the building clouds. "It moving in fast. Remember last storm?"

"All too well," said Molly, not really wanting to remember. It would serve no purpose to think again of her outburst and how she had been so short tempered with the Doc.

"Da," said Mrs. Kaposhkin, "that was the night that the Wilson baby died."

"What?" said Molly. "That baby died?"

"Da," she said again. "Why you not know that, Molly? Doc was with them."

"How could that be?" she asked, her voice unsure.

"Mr. Wilson he came and he find Doc on beach. Doc waiting to see if any survivors of wreck." She was standing at the helm, her hands on the wheel, ready to change direction. "Mr. Wilson, he know everyone was down at Bluffs with shipwreck. Doc he go with Mr. Wilson, he do everything but baby too frail to live. Did you not help deliver baby that night?" she asked.

"Yes, I helped to deliver the baby but I didn't know the Doc had to go back there. I didn't know that's where he was. I thought he left the beach to do his drinking."

"Come about," yelled Mrs. K. Molly ducked as the boom swung over. "We head back to Island Molly. We not go to mainland today." A sudden chill enveloped them. It was the head of a cold front pushing through. The wind snapped the lines and billowed out the sail. The sun disappeared all too quickly as the storm clouds, tumbling over each other, moved in to fill up the sky. Even the color of the water changed. What had been a deep blue green changed to an inky foreboding black.

"We make a run for it," said Mrs. K, in a voice louder then she had intended. "Maybe wind come 'round and blow us in. We be too far out," she mumbled. "Extra sweaters in hold, Molly Anne, you go get. We be in for some weather," she said raising her voice to be heard. In no time, icy particles began blowing through the air, stinging their cheeks while salt spray danced through the air.

"We heading back home," said Madam Kaposhkin, dropping her unlit pipe in her apron pocket. "No chance we make mainland today." Molly knew not to argue. No one knew the sea better than Mrs. K. "Look like strong squall line, we gonna be in for a blow. I not paying attention, too much running my mouth," she said as she pulled on her thick wool mittens. They warmed her fingers almost instantly. They were matted just the way she liked them from years of being soaked and drying in sun. Not the way wool was usually treated, but necessary if they were to be waterproof and able to withstand the frigid New England weather.

"Here Molly Anne," she said, passing her a pair that she pulled out of her apron pocket. "Nothing better for keeping weather out. Sheep's wool is best yet. Keep warm air in and cold air out." Molly obediently pulled on the thick mittens, grateful for the protection they provided.

"We get our bearings here and we head straight in. Molly, take the wheel, I go down in cabin, get oil skins on."

"But the wind, we're heeling over so." she yelled, feeling the sharp breeze tearing at her cape threatening to rip it off.

"You be fine, you been through storms before."

Reluctantly Molly took the wheel. "Good girl, hold straight on course, I be right back."

Molly squinted into the flying spray, trying to see through the grayness of the storm. The boat was tossed and thrown about like a cork, as she struggled to keep her balance.

"Mrs. K," she suddenly screamed, "quick, come quick." She squinted to the west in disbelief. A huge rogue wave from out of nowhere was bearing down on them, a wall of water nearly sucking out the air she was breathing, blotting out everything else.

"Help," she screeched.

The old woman popped back up out of the cabin, looking at Molly, her lips forming the word "What..." Her eyes widened in disbelief. It was hard not to miss the powerful wave building up behind them. She was across the deck in two long strides, grabbing the wheel, forcing it around to meet the wave head on. Molly had heard of waves like this, but had never encountered one; in fact she'd thought they were just part of the yarns that fishermen liked to spin on a cold winter night. But here it was.

Molly was thrown like a bit of refuse on the deck as she released the wheel. The wave towered over them, the roar nearly deafening. As the boat swung around the boom flew from one side to the other. The old woman never even saw it as it slammed into her back. There was a horrid crack as she was knocked, face down, onto the slippery deck. The water crashed across the deck sweeping everything into the sea. Everything except one young girl and one aged and now silent woman.

~

~ CHAPTER THIRTEEN ~

The ancient Russian had been knocked unconscious. Molly yanked off her thick mittens and slid them under the silent woman's head, then mopped at her face with the hem of her cape. She secured the ship's wheel, to keep the small craft heading in the direction of the harbor. Speaking quiet words she tried to bring her around. It was moments only but felt like hours when her eyes fluttered open. "Molly Anne, I not gonna make it, you know I not going to."

"Mrs. K., you'll be alright. Hang on. Help will come." The storm had passed as quickly as it had sprung up. The boat rocked gently as the waves lapped against the sides. The sail hung limp. Water sloshed on the cabin floor.

"Molly Anne, it be my time," she said. Her

voice was soft. "I been taking up enough space in world. It time for others. Let them have their turn. I go meet my Stanley." She coughed a hard rasping cough, wincing as the pain shot up her shattered back.

"You can't say that," Molly said. "You can't leave me. Who will I have? There's no one out there..."

"Molly Anne," she interrupted, nearly breathless, "there is someone. Listen to me now, I tell you story that happen long time ago." She let out a great sigh then started again. "Maybe sixteen years ago. It happen before you were born." Molly rubbed at her eyes trying to clear the salt spray with the sleeve of her dress. "I be needing a drink, if you please," she said, her voice fading. "There be a mite of rum in flask under mattress."

Her eyes closed as she drew in a few breaths of the icy air as Molly disappeared into the cabin.

"Thank you child," she said as she sipped from the flask that Molly held out to her. Muted sunlight glistened off the tarnished silver. She coughed again.

"It was summer," she said, "late in summer. Your Grams and Pap wanted sail to mainland.

They want to take daughter to see Doctor in Providence. She not well, she feeling poorly." Molly thought for a moment that the ancient fisherwoman had died, her breathing was so shallow, but then her eyes fluttered open, searching for just a moment, trying to focus. "This daughter, her name Charity Mott. Is good name. We cross channel very easily, ocean smooth like glass, some breeze, not much. Charity sick. Sick whole way over. Your Grams and Pap very upset, very concerned. Charity so pale, so thin. But cape fell open."

She paused again and Molly held the flask to her lips. "Thank you child," she said pausing another moment. "Weather not cold. Not like this. No need for cape. I saw the bulge she want to hide. I knew." She rested a moment trying to catch her breath. "Your Grams and Pap," she began again, "Make me promise, this was a secret. There is no one I tell. Not hard. Islanders not like me only you family like me." Her breathing had become very shallow.

"My family?" she asked.

"Da, Molly Anne, that was your family," she paused again. "Charity, she was your mumma." Her eyes would not stay open. She appeared to fall into a deep sleep. Molly wanted to shake her to make her tell more. It was just moments when her eyes fluttered open again. She looked around curiously as if trying to remember where she was, then she focused on Molly, and her face softened.

"Your Grams and Pap," she said, "They stay on the mainland for a month, maybe more, then Charity she die." Each word seemed to be wrung out of her.

Is that the end of the story Molly thought, watching the wrinkled eyes close again? Molly stood, her knees creaking from kneeling in the cramped cockpit. She stood staring at the vast horizon trying to absorb what she'd just been told. Was that true? Grams and Pap really were her grandparents. A feeling of warmth washed over her with the good memories that she had of them and then equally as quickly were pushed aside as she once again remembered how sorely she'd missed them and their kind and loving ways. She'd belonged there. It was the only place she'd ever belonged.

"Molly Anne." She turned and looked down at the tortured face of the ancient fisher woman. "Molly Anne," she said again. "More. Come here please." She knelt back down on the slippery deck, beside the old woman. "There is father. You have father." Molly smiled down at her faithful friend of all these years.

"Of course."

"No, Molly Anne, he here. He be on the Island." Molly wondered if she'd heard right, then afraid to imagine which of the tough and burly fishermen it could be. Maybe it was best if she didn't know.

"Your father," she continued, "He went away to school on mainland. He be very young. He know nothing about you. Your Grams and Pap thought to tell him when he return, but it never happened." She coughed a painful long hacking cough, at the end a trickle of blood slid out from the corner of her mouth. Molly gently dabbed at it with the hem of her skirt. The ancient eyes closed again, pain etched across her brow. Molly was sure she was sleeping as she rose to find her a blanket. The old woman's gnarled hand reached out for her. "Nyet, do not go. I must tell you everything. I promise your Grams and Pap if anything happen to them that I watch out for you." She paused again, her breath labored. "Molly Anne, your father, he came back to island."

~

~ CHAPTER FOURTEEN ~

The boat rocked gently in the calming sea with no one to guide it.

"He came back?" asked Molly, looking down on the Russian who was taking only the shallowest of breaths. Back from where? She thought quickly, who had returned to the island after a long absence. She gasped. Her hand flew up to her mouth. "No," she said looking down at the injured woman. Madam Kaposhkin looked up at her with eyes that appeared to stare at her through a thinning fog.

"Da, Molly Anne. The Doctor. Your father. He not know this," she said, her breathing shallow. "I hoping you two get along, without my having to tell him. I want to tell him many times and I try, but he won't listen." She sighed. "You,

Molly Anne, you look like your mumma. Your father so in love with her. Your Grams and Pap thought maybe they married while on mainland, but no one know this."

"They said when he hear she die, he say he never again set foot on Island. He get caught up in war. But after war, he wander and wander, not find a place to settle."

It was too much for her, even though she struggled to keep her eyes open. Her heavy lids slid slowly over the nearly unseeing eyes. Molly watched as she slipped into a deep sleep, her breathing became more regular. Tucking the blanket around her, she again wiped at the thin trickle of blood that escaped from between reddened lips. The shredded canvas of what had once been a sail flapped untethered in the breeze.

Molly stood and for a moment rubbed at the creak in her back. She couldn't think about what she'd been told. It could not be imagined. Put it out of my mind she thought – How could it be true. She went down into the cabin to find the patched sail that Mrs. K. had so recently repaired. She would replace the shredded canvas with the one that had been tended to and carefully mended and head for home.

~

They sailed towards the protected harbor, easily running ahead of the light wind. A thousand thoughts raced through her mind but she had to get help for Madam Kaposhkin. Untangling the canvas that had been ripped nearly to shreds after the wild storm, she deftly raised the recently patched sail then guided the small double-ender back to its home. A lone seagull watched from its place high in the sky as it trailed behind them, its wings stretched out, letting its feathered body glide effortlessly in the breeze.

Molly looked up, shading her eyes from the setting sun. "Hello Mr. Seagull. Are you guiding us back to our home?" Almost as if he heard her he answered with one lonely cry heard only by the occupants of the solitary boat.

Jim Bone appeared from nowhere, pulling alongside the battered boat. His strong arms pulled at the oars of his sturdy skiff. He met Molly's eyes. She nodded as if to say thank you. His oars continued to dip in and out of the water as he guided them safely back to the harbor.

Squinting into the distance, she was not surprised to see there was a small crowd waiting on the dock. The town watched out for its own, she knew, and if one of the fishing boats was missing or overdue the word always spread quickly.

With Jim Bone's help, she guided the small boat up to the dock and threw the line to one of the fishermen. She saw Jack standing a little apart from the rest of the crowd. Madam Kaposhkin, visible for all to see was lying unconscious, stretched out on the floor of the cockpit. Molly's thick mittens formed a pillow for her head, a blanket pulled up nearly to her chin.

"Go get the Doctor, go on now and run," Jack said over his shoulder to his younger brother. "And be quick about it." Mack dashed off startling the gulls that had been standing vigil, strangely silent. Jack ran over and grabbed hold of the gunnel, steadying the boat.

"Molly, you all right?" he asked, concern furrowed his brow and clouded the deep brown of his eyes. Not waiting for an answer, he leaped down from the pier, landing lightly on the deck of the boat.

"Fine," she said, but shook her head when

she looked down at the very still, barely breathing woman. "But I'm not so sure about Mrs. K.," she said. "It's her back." There was little they could do. Molly tucked in a stray corner of the blanket and dabbed gently at the thin trickle of blood that seeped down from the corner of her mouth.

Two of the fishermen had jumped in and worked to lower the sail, tying it with the lines. They fussed unnecessarily over each detail of securing the boat while trying to stay out of the way.

Jack retied the line, trying to find something to do while Molly again straightened the blanket covering the still woman. Both wondering if the Doctor would really come, knowing it would be difficult to move the prostrate woman. "We'll wait," said Jack. "I'm sure he'll be along."

The fishermen on the dock milled about quietly, knowing a tragedy had taken place, speaking among themselves in near whispers.

Molly could hear bits of the quiet conversation as they looked down into the boat. "She was good. We liked her." One after another walked by with a shy nod or a few quiet words.

"Molly," said Jack, "here he comes." Molly

looked up. He was easy to spot with the worn out cape that nearly swallowed him up. Not quite sure how she should act with her new knowledge, she looked over at Mrs. Kaposhkin who began to stir.

Molly leaned over. "The Doctor is coming, hang on," she said as she reached down to touch the kindly old face. Molly felt the boat tip as he stepped aboard. He glanced over at Molly. Was it a hurt expression or one that was resigned? He nodded at her then knelt next to the barely breathing woman.

The day had warmed, but still she felt cold. She pulled the sleeves of her dress down trying to cover the tips of her fingers. She let Jack take her elbow to help her off the boat. He squeezed her arm, saying nothing.

The fishermen nodded to her and one by one almost as if prearranged came up to her and said a kind word as they reached out their work worn hands and either touched her arm or her elbow. Jake, the oldest fisherman of the group, was only able to do a quick, "Sorry." Antonio was behind him. He'd never said more to Mrs. K than "How's it goin'?" But now he said, "Too bad for her, she was one of the best," Art Buckman said. "Sorry."

Another said, "She's a good woman," and another, "You did well." And, of course, always in the middle of any event; Mrs. Littlefield kept up with her "Oh my. Oh my," as she paced back and forth, her fingers held close to her mouth as if trying to stop the words from coming.

Together they stood looking down into the cockpit. Molly was hardly aware of the tears that trailed down her reddened cheeks as the Doctor gently ministered to her friend. She saw him speaking to her now and again and watched as he leaned over to hear what she said. Once after listening for many minutes, he looked up into the faces staring at him and found Molly's. An ever so slight smile played at the corners of his lips, while a nearly incredulous look passed over his eyes as they searched her face.

It seemed forever but perhaps wasn't more than an hour or two when they saw the Doctor remove his cherished, ragged cape and gently place it over the old fisherwoman, easily covering all of her from the top of her head to her feet.

For just a moment he stood and looked down at her. Then slowly, using his good arm, he saluted, either to the cape or to the dead woman or both. No one was quite sure. He packed up the tools he had used, fumbling less than usual.

Molly watched his every move. He stood. He was tall and straight, his shoulders pulled back giving him more height. His bushy beard almost looked tame. Hopping off the boat, he walked confidently across the pier. Molly's breath caught in her throat as she watched him, his long stride taking him to the end of the pier. He was nearly passed where she stood. He stopped. Jack released his hold on her.

He stood for just a moment, his deep blue eyes searching hers, saying nothing, as though searching for words. Then, "I'm sorry," he said, looking deep within her. "Come home. Come home where you belong."

She released the tight hold her fingers had on the sleeves of her dress, her fingers now warmed by the protection of the woolen fabric. Putting his wounded, but healed arm around her shoulders, he led her off the Island pier towards home.

~ THE END ~

~ ABOUT THE AUTHOR ~

Tecla Emerson was born in Lexington, Massachusetts and went on to live in Boston, Plymouth and other towns in the New England area. Currently living in Annapolis, she is the publisher and editor of *OutLook by the Bay*, a regional magazine. She is the author of many other young reader chapter books and can be reached at TeclaEmerson@gmail.com

~ BLOCK ISLAND FACTOIDS ~

- Originally the home of the Niantic Indians, Block Island was first seen by Giovanni de Verrazzano in 1524. The Island was later settled by Europeans after Dutch explorer Adrian Block visited in 1614.

- A double ender was a boat unique to Block Island in the 17th and 18th century. Constructed on the Island, the boat provided extra stability, a plus in the unpredictable waters of New England.

- The Island, just short of 10 square miles, is located 13 miles from the coast of Rhode Island.

- Today, a short ferry ride across Block Island Sound from Rhode Island or Long Island, N.Y. takes residents and visitors to the Island.

- Currently inhabited by just over 1,000 year round residents, it is a favorite destination for tourists.

- Block Island was originally a farming and fishing village that depended on an income from their catch of cod, mackerel, haddock and other local fish that the fishing boats brought in.

- During the 1800s two lighthouses were constructed on the Island to aid mariners through the surrounding, often unpredictable waters. Both have been extensively renovated and have been moved further inland from their precarious locations at the ocean's edge.

- Irish moss, also known as carrageen, is a seaweed that can be found on the rocky coast of the Atlantic Ocean. Once used as an ingredient in pudding and a cosmetic cream, it is now used as a thickening agent and considered by some to be a nutritious supplement.

~ SOURCES ~

A History of Block Island: From Its Discovery, in 1514, to the Present Time, 1876 (Classic Reprint) By S.T. Livermore, Forgotten Books 2012

Block Island and Long Island by Dorothy Sterling and Winifred Lubell, W.W. Norton & Company, 1992

Block Island: An Illustrated Guide (Classic Reprint) By Beatrice Ball, Forgotten books, 2017

Block Island: Lore and Legends by Ethel Colt Ritchie, Mrs. Frances M. Nugent; 10th edition, 1980

Legends and Stories from Martha's Vineyard, Nantucket and Block Island, by John Halsted, Abela Publishing, 2014

The Outer Lands: A Natural History Guide to Cape Cod, Martha's Vineyard, Nantucket, Block Island, and Long Island, by Dorothy Sterling

ANTIETAM - WAKING THE FURY

Emily at 15 is bored and annoyed with just about everything and everybody. Tired of her chores and irritated by the endless care of three younger sisters, she would like to have a life of her own. Her parents are absent; her Father is off fighting a war she doesn't understand and her Mother has left for Pennsylvania. As the eldest of the four sisters, she must take responsibility for her home and family. When the bloodiest battle of the Civil War is fought almost on her doorstep she is unwillingly pressed into service. Emily is called on to make decisions and to take charge of wounded soldiers while fending off the invading troops and protecting her younger sisters. Life changes forever as she discovers a courage that she did not know she possessed. Strengths emerge as she stands up for her beliefs while sheltering the enemy and caring for a runaway slave, both of which hold very serious consequences. In this remarkably accurate depiction of the Battle of Antietam, a legend is once more uncovered. It involves a mass of very angry bees. This dangerous, stinging swarm may well have had an influence on the outcome of that fateful day in 1862.

Now available at Amazon, Apple, Nook (Barnes and Noble), Kobo and other online retailers in print and digital editions!

THE LETTER

"My being forever banished from your sight..."

Just who was this "...undut-iful and Disobedient Child" who in 1756 penned a letter to her father in England?

What had she done to so offend him?

Why, as an extremely well-educated young girl, had she become an indentured servant? Why was she alone? In her letter, she pleads with her father to forgive her and to at least send her a bit of clothing. "...almost naked, no shoes nor stockings to wear."

Here, within these pages, the mystery of Elizabeth Sprigs is revealed. It is a tale based on a single letter sent from Baltimore so long ago.

Now available at Amazon, Apple, Nook (Barnes and Noble), Kobo and other online retailers in print and digital editions!

JENNIE WADE:
A GIRL FROM GETTYSBURG

It had been foolish to stay but now there was no choice. It was anyone's guess what the outcome would be. Nothing was as it should be. Oddly, the Confederate troops were pouring in from the north and Union troops were marching in from the south. They arrived in droves. The town was not prepared for what happened during the early days of the summer, 1863. Jennie, a young local girl, did her best to keep up with the demand for bread and water and medical care for the troops. Her brothers were scattered, her sister would soon be having a baby, her mother was not bearing up well and Jack, her intended, had not been heard from in weeks. It was a time and place that would be recorded in American history forever. A time marked by the largest number of casualties in the Civil War. It was Gettysburg, Pennsylvania, a small, unremarkable town; an easily forgotten town that would live in infamy and one that history would never forget. Of the almost 50,000 casualties of that encounter in early July, only one civilian was killed. This is her story. The story of Jennie Wade, a dedicated young woman thrown into the middle of one of Americans' most tragic times.

Now available at Amazon, Apple, Nook (Barnes and Noble), Kobo and other online retailers in print and digital editions!

MISTS OF THE BLUE RIDGE

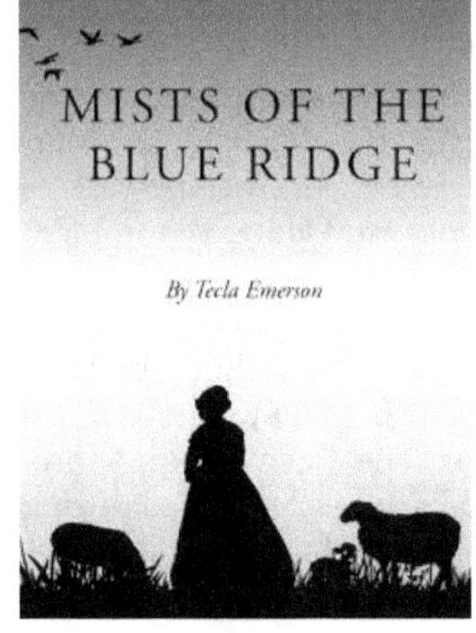

Olivia lived a quiet and protected life tucked away on a farm in the Blue Ridge Mountains. It was far from the great war that had been raging between the North and the South. She had little interest in the who and the why of it all, and wasn't even sure where her sympathies lay. Then, without warning, the conflict surrounded her. At 16, she was ill prepared for the responsibilities that were thrust on her.

This is her story. It's a tale that tells of courage, determination and survival during one of America's most trying times.

Now available at Amazon, Apple, Nook (Barnes and Noble), Kobo and other online retailers in print and digital editions!

HIDDEN IN THE EARLY LIGHT
A TALE OF THE IRISH FAMINE

Katy was 16 when the hard times came. Her father disappeared in the night and her mother left her with a tiny baby sister. She was suddenly thrust into the role of caretaker. It was a responsibility she didn't want. The farming life was not for her and now she had to find a way to survive and to keep her younger brothers from starving. How could she ever be free of a life she hadn't chosen?

It was the 1840s and thousands were dying from the great potato famine, one of history's most dreadful events.

This is Katy's story, the story of how a young girl survived by using her wits, determination and courage.

www.ingramcontent.com/pod-product-compliance
Lightning Source LLC
Chambersburg PA
CBHW070401200726

48294CB00003B/1028